HANSEN'S CHIL

Ognjen Spahić was born in Podgorica, Montenegro in 1977, where he still lives and works as Cultural Correspondent for the independent newspaper *Vijesti*. He is one in a group of dynamic, award-winning new writers who have left behind the constraints of the old system and are putting down strong roots in their new democracies.

Spahić has published two collections of short stories: *All That*, 2001 and *Winter Search*, 2007. *Hansen's Children* won the prestigious Meša Selimović Prize upon its original publication in 2005, and went on to win the Ovid Festival Prize, 2011. Up till now, it has been published in seven European languages.

First published in 2011 by

Istros Books
Conway Hall
25 Red Lion Square
London
WC1R 4RL
United Kingdom
www.istrosbooks.com

Printed in England by
ImprintDigital, Exeter EX5 5HY

Cover photo and design: Roxana Stere

Second edition published May, 2012
ISBN: 978-1-908236-08-1

This edition has been made possible with the help of the Ministry of Culture of Montenegro

Hansen's Children

Ognjen Spahić

Translated from the original Montenegrin by Will Firth

Introduction by Nick Thorpe

Hansen's children really do exist, but in a world much softened by the impact of the Romanian revolution: the small hamlet of Tichilesti in the Danube Delta. There, Vasile prunes his vines with fingers that feel almost nothing, but he remembers well what his legless father, calling to him from the edge of the vineyard, taught him when he was twelve years old. Vasile's vines and wines help the inmates of Europe's last lepers' colony stay sane – alongside the medication that doctors and nurses administer to them daily. Across the valley, Ioana is well into her 80s, and chops the grass to feed her hens with a little blunt axe gripped between the two stumps of wrists where her hands once were. She calls each of her hens by name; there is even one called Scumpa ('the limper'). Ioana's simple pleasures, when I last visited in springtime, consisted of watching her tomato plants grow, each in its little yoghurt pot, and looking forward to nursing them to fruit in her little garden. 'Everyone praises them,' she told me, 'as the sweetest in the whole colony!'

Further down the valley, Costica is now completely blind. (Leprosy affects each of its victims in a different way.) His good eye exploded, he tells me matter-of-factly, during the 1989 revolution, and he humorously even suggests a link: so much was blowing up at that time, he seems to be saying, so why not his remaining eye as well? The radio next to his couch keeps him in touch with the outside world – more than that, it is his companion day and night, preventing him from sinking into total oblivion.

Ognjen Spahić lifts the leprosarium – gently but firmly, and with a poet's sensitivity to ugliness as well as beauty – out of the present, placing it back in the nightmare world of Ceausescu's Romania only a few months before the Revolution that would change everything forever. In doing so, he transforms the lepers and their affliction into an allegory for the outcasts, the aliens, the afflicted throughout time. Leprosy might be AIDS, it might be the Black Death, or it might simply be what makes any minority different from – and hated by – the majority. But his is not a romantic view of an accursed group worthy of our respect. Rather, it is a nightmarish vision of the depths to which a community can sink when its members turn on one another. As such, it echoes William Golding's *Lord of the Flies* – but in this case, it is a grown-up world where all outside constraints are relaxed, not one of children.

Spahić's bloodbath mirrors another: that of the Romanian revolution, and by extension, that of the French revolution or the Russian revolution. However, as a Montenegrin and a former inmate of the great leprosarium of Yugoslavia, Spahić's allegory – and his nightmare – venture much deeper. As a young author growing up in a country literally tearing itself apart limb from limb, he turns his imagination loose upon an east Balkan leprosarium to produce a Frankenstein worthy of the Kosovan war, the Macedonian or the Croatian, or (God forbid) even of the Bosnian war. But he has still not finished. The survivors of his leprosarium – all two of them – travel upriver to infect the rest of Europe in a deeply dark vision of the wickedness of both the majority and the minority. The novel is a worthy challenge for all of us to think differently about human nature.

The real lepers of Tichilesti – the last 19 of them, from a population that once reached nearly 200 – stay there not because they have to, but because of the companionship they have come to feel for one another after a lifetime of living together. Many were born there to leper mothers and fathers, inheriting the disease (as Spahić has correctly chronicled). They grew up alongside one another; some dared to believe for a while that they were not infected. When the telltale signs emerged, however, they ended up at Tichilesti once again – and once they were trapped there, as Spahić relates, they could not leave. Yet here reality dissents from fiction. Nicolae Ceausescu, Romania's demented dictator from 1965 to 1989, didn't want the outside world to know of the existence of a disease that his peculiarly national breed of Communism was unable to cure – all the more strongly because his wife Elena owed her position in the Romanian Communist Party, and her own cult of personality as First Lady, to her carefully cultivated prestige as 'the Scientist': a title designed to appeal, no doubt, to those who might have been offended by the status of her clumsy husband, the son of a lowly cobbler.

Like HIV/AIDS, leprosy is not an illness that can be contracted 'casually' with a simple shake of the hand, in vivid contrast to the fears expressed by Spahić's glove-wearing characters. The medicines distributed by the doctors and nurses of Tichilesti – themselves absent from Spahić's portrayal – turn the illness back on itself after a very brief period of infection. The medicines prevent leprosy's contagion, but can only slow down its effects, unable to reverse its impact on the bodies of victims. Another strange fact about leprosy is that for decades, animals remained immune to the best efforts of scientists to infect them with it, though there has been slightly more success in the past few decades with the use of nude mice and nine-banded armadillos. It is now treated – in Romania, as throughout the world – with a combination of three drugs: rifampicin, dapsone, and clofazimine.

There is no fertiliser factory next to the real leprosarium; anyway, it would not be visible from most of the individual houses in this protected valley where the last lepers while out their final years on Earth. However, there were plenty of fertiliser factories in Ceausescu's Romania, in Milosevic's Serbia, and in Honecker's German Democratic Republic. Spahić's brutal portrayals are not figments of a diseased imagination, but of a healthy one; they share much in common with the brutalities of Srebrenica, of Stolac, of Rwanda, of Abu Ghraib, of Darfur and of Homs.

In the second decade of the twenty-first century, the last lepers stay in the colony at Tichilesti not because they have to, but because they want to: they grew up here, fell in love with each other here, fought one another here, and buried each other here. They would feel strange living anywhere else, although they cherish their brief trips to the outside world along with every gesture, every glance, every refusal to stare that suggests that they too are ordinary – are real, are as unblemished, are as equal as we all are in death. 'Never forget,' admonished the much underrated British writer and essayist Theodore Powys, 'that Death, whenever it comes, to whomever it comes, is always a blessing.'

Read Ognjen Spahić's remarkable, beautiful, horrible parody of Europe, your Europe, my Europe – and tremble.

Nick Thorpe, Tbilisi, Georgia, April 2012

Nick Thorpe is the BBC's East and Central European Correspondent and has reported from the region since 1986.

'With the slow snow the lepers descend'

René Char, in his poem 'Victory Lightning'

Europe's last home for lepers, or leprosarium, is located in south-eastern Romania amidst the leprous landscapes of dark, barren soil, scarred by the smokestacks of power stations and the remnants of once mighty forests. Long have the fertile clods disappeared that recalled the heavy footsteps of Burebista and Decebalus, the Dacian princes ever ready to sink iron into the glistening flanks of Roman horses and the bellies of Trajan's strapping, well-fed legionaries. Later Vlad III, the Impaler, Prince Mircea the Old, Stephen the Great of Moldavia, the 'Athlete of Christ', and Michael the Brave (all devoted apostles of the word of God) were like stars in the black night that Christendom looked up to with hope when Ottoman scimitars spilt rivers of young blood.

Throughout history, as people like to recall, this country has been torn apart by the claws of evil old lions, their grizzled manes spattered with the gore of subjugated millions.

But Romania has not forgotten the glory of the brave. Rivers flow past, but rocks remain, as a Romanian saying goes, and even today tales are told of the exploits of Prince Vlad's heroic legions that devoted their last ounce of strength to their native land.

My dear room-mate, Robert W. Duncan, has a habit of saying that history is the third eye of humanity and that it allows us to perceive more clearly the pitfalls of our melancholic age. I always reply by citing Emil Cioran who wrote, 'if there were no such thing as melancholy, people would roast and eat nightingales'. Robert says he is horrified by the very thought of plucked nightingale garnished with mint and garlic, and begs me not to mention the painful notion again. I begin to chirp through my missing teeth, flap my arms and flutter around the room until Robert grabs his slippers and flings them at my head. He wants to sleep. I cannot.

I like to stand at the window on dry summer evenings and feel the tiny fragments of history, only recently turned to dust, fall on my bare head in the fresh breeze from the Carpathians or the warmer one that blows steadily down the rocky slopes of the Transylvanian Alps. I smell the forests and the whortleberry, the breath of lush fields and the flower of the dwarf lilac bush; the taste of the stones, whose particles grit between my teeth and stab at the delicate veil of my cataract. When I close my right eye, which is healthy and full of life, a curtain of mist descends on the landscape; the moon becomes squashed chewing gum and my room-mate a dozing rat. The violet lights of the nearby fertiliser factory flicker like dying stars, while the bronze bust of King Alexander John I in the middle of the leprosarium courtyard hardly seems to be there. I open my right eye and close the left. I open and close them in turn, enjoying my own private dualism of the world.

The pages that follow are written as seen through the right eye and with the involvement of all my rational, conscious being.

The people I met and got to know on my road (you will appreciate that I cannot say anything first-hand about Burebista and Decebalus, or King John) will be described as my conscience dictates. Those I did not meet but who by design or chance have become an indelible part of my life, will be transformed into words to the best of my ability, and I shall take care that not one printed letter scar the full beauty of the truth.

CHAPTER ONE

On 16 April 1989, I got up before the others. I planned to pick some of the still unopened daffodils that grew along the southern wall of the leprosarium. I wanted them to flower in my room, so I went down the two sets of stairs from the second floor with a tin brim-full of water. The evening before, the tin had been full of pineapple rings which Robert and I had savoured. The tins of pineapple regularly escaped the attention of the customs officials and hungry Romanian villagers, who would flog any foodstuffs of value when aid packages came from the International Red Cross. Only the tins of this juicy tropical fruit would be left at the bottom of the boxes, presumably due to some food-related superstition like 'coffee from South Africa is radioactive' or 'New Zealand apples are artificially coloured'.

It was a pleasure to look out at the snowy slopes of the distant mountains and think of the hands of the Caribbean girls, which just a few months earlier had caressed the coarse skin of the fruit we were relishing the heart of. As we devoured our pineapple, in our thoughts we licked the palms of those tender hands, and I am not ashamed to say that I often ended up with a slight erection.

Rays of the early sun were tenderly piercing the tall plume of smoke from the fertiliser factory. Daffodils are best picked before the sun rises: that way you catch them asleep, petals closed, and can shift them to a different bed. The cold water makes them stay fresh for several weeks and they open every morning. I picked them by breaking the stems a centimetre above the ground, taking care not to damage the large bulb that held many more yellow flowers for the years to come, for the graves that would hold the leprous bones of my friends.

Since 1981 we had been confined to the leprosarium so as to reduce the costs of transport to the crematorium in Bucharest and avoid sending urns to families throughout Europe. This change did not prompt any great protest, I recall, because all of us lepers (now I've said it!) spent our days here due to those same relatives' dread of our ancient illness. Leprosy most commonly conjures up two things in people's minds: firstly, scenes from William Wyler's Ben Hur, where a colony of lepers is shown roaming the earth as if punished by God, doomed to contempt and a painful death in lonely caves far from the city; and secondly, fear of a biological aberration that a fatal mistake of nature, or perhaps divine justice, had let blunder into our modern age.

They believed that our pale gnarled flesh, the bulging growths on our backs, arms, and necks, contained spores of the disease just waiting to waft out and democratically disseminate this oldest of all diseases. Dull-witted Romanian villagers, their minds decayed by irrational fears and superstitions, considered us outcasts, pariahs of humanity, and also evil. They even forbade their ugly children from playing within hundreds of metres of the leprosarium fence.

I always had the impression that our building and its immediate surroundings were seen more as a haunted graveyard teeming with evil spirits than as a medical institution. I suppose this was compounded by the long linen garments we wore: necessary protection from the sun and the gazes of other lepers. Of those who had eyes, at least.

Every leper wants to know how the bodies of the others are disfigured. This is a standard topic of private conversation among them; a morbid show-and-tell of what they lack. The most sensitive spot are the male genitals, which in some stages of the disease closely resemble dried gentian root or an old man's crooked and impotent fingers. The health of this body part tacitly determined a person's status in the colony.

I had the rare fortune that my masculinity remained untouched by the 'marvels' of Gerhard Armauer Hansen's bacillus. Since I was endowed with quite decent dimensions before contracting the disease, soon after arrival your narrator was ascribed the status of leader - for what it was worth.

Whenever it was time to share out the alms that the Catholic community had left for us at the gate, estimate the amount of firewood needed or divide a crop of potatoes or cherries into fair parts, I was called on to preside. Usually everything went off without any problems. Either there were no complaints, or no one had the strength to complain. Protest was limited to mutterings under linen hoods or minor squabbles in the dark corridors of the building. But sometimes things got out of hand and required radical measures in agreement with the other residents. One time Cion Eminescu clobbered Mstislaw Kasiewicz on the head with a large piece of firewood, all because of a misunderstanding about the size of the tomatoes they had been given. That demanded a swift and just reaction.

Grudgingly I unlocked the door to Room 42, a cellar which by consensus could be used as a lock-up to sanction unacceptable behaviour. It was only used four times in all my years at the leprosarium. Poor Cion spent the night he deserved in there, and the next morning too: being punished had offended him and he refused to come out. When Mstislaw generously offered to relinquish his share of the juicy red orbs, Cion came out sobbing; the former enemies fell into each other's arms and everything returned to normal.

Mstislaw's and Cion's warm embraces were later exchanged in the intimacy of high-ceilinged rooms, on mattresses filled with mouldy wool, in the bathrooms and dead-end corridors of the leprosarium. I never understood how they overcame the disfigurement of their disease-riddled bodies. Cion had no nose; instead there was a gaping hole, dark and mucousy, into which you could stick at least two fingers. Nor was the rest of him particularly attractive. His right leg, without the foot, dragged on the ground behind him like a corpse, while exceptionally large lumps of hardened flesh lifted the linen robe off his back.

Mstislaw suffered from a different form of mutilation. His facial features were all intact, but the disease affected the joints of every limb. This gave him a gait reminiscent of the movements of a monstrous marionette from a child's darkest nightmares. Whatever the sexual relationship of these two unfortunates was like, I am sure Mstislaw was never on his knees.

The first complaints about their affair began for reasons that were exceedingly pragmatic and equally ridiculous. Issue 36 of the Medical Gazette (January 1984), published in Bucharest under the auspices of the United Nations, pompously announced 'a new disease that would change the face of the earth'. In the next few days everyone read the pages about 'Autoimmune Deficiency Syndrome', some with a sneer, others with calm incomprehension. The advent of this new pestilence also instilled a degree of envy, I noted. You could tell that leprosy was held in strange awe by its victims. Bitter debates ensued in the courtyard, senseless statements were made, full of scorn and hatred; some claimed that AIDS was a medical farce designed to detract from the acknowledged scourges of humanity: the plague, cancer, syphilis, and of course leprosy. They loved their disease and respected it as a worthy opponent.

'AIDS primarily affects intravenous drug-users, haemophiliacs and homosexuals', Ingemar Zoltán read out, while the others nodded with an air of importance and exchanged whispers in which, not surprisingly, the names Cion and Mstislaw were heard. With this new knowledge, attitudes to the two lovers changed considerably. The nature of the new disease was misunderstood and homosexual acts per se were seen as spawning the new evil. Mstislaw and Cion were shunned... like lepers. It was kind of understandable.

Those who are not familiar with the subtle moods of the deformed leprous body and mind will find it hard to understand lepers' seemingly irrational behaviour. These are often rooted in motivations foreign to those of you from that other world – the world of non-lepers. It was the same mechanism that caused the excommunication of Cion and Mstislaw, but this was obscured by the commotion about 'the new disease' and its alleged apostles: the homosexuals.

Over the years the reality of leprosy gave rise to the rule that emotions were impossible and forbidden in the leprosarium: we were all one body that lived the disease, slept the disease, and died of it. This practical arrangement, if I may be so bold, could be considered part of the natural equilibrium that aims to preserve the fragile physical and mental health of the human race.

Degeneration of the penis did away with reproductive instincts and the possibility of pregnancies within the community of lepers.

In the leprosarium, together with eleven men, there was almost one woman. I phrase it in that way because the only woman, the elderly Russian Margareta Yosipovich, vegetated in a state of semi-hibernation from as early as I can remember. She did not leave her room for years on end, but Death did not yet want to call for her. I was the only one who visited; knocking on her door once a week, I waited patiently for her vocal chords to utter a barely audible mumble, before I would go in to take her pulse and spoon some soup into her mouth. Margareta would reply with stories, memories that went back to the last days of tsarist Russia and the cruel gulags of the Siberian tundra, but also to the early history of the leprosarium shortly after it was founded.

Her rasping voice came from deep inside, its low frequencies filling the room. After ten minutes I felt it was coming from all around. She spoke fluently and in a steady tone reminiscent of an old gramophone record.

Her Russian sometimes drove me crazy. She would speak about the tsarist period using an assortment of archaic terms and exotic adjectives, which completely undermined my high-school Russian. When she spoke of Red Russia it was like a parade of presumptuous names of different committees and titles of minor Stalinist officials. It was thanks to them, if I got it right, that she and her husband froze their butts off in Siberia for years on end. And it was there, in Gulag 32-A, that Margareta contracted Hansen's bacillus in return for her labours. Broken by the heavy burden of leprosy, this courageous woman managed to stay healthy in mind up until the very end. Margareta had abandoned her body, consciously discharging it and hoping for the compassion of her fellow lepers. She had spent the last ten years afloat on a black sea of memories, constantly complaining of the cold, the Siberian cold, that dwelt evermore in her skull.

My torment, and that of the others, began at daybreak. A line of blue workers' aprons filed off to work, and you were faced with a day full of pain of varying intensity. Your communication with the rest of the world usually began with looking to see if there were any new changes to your body. Depending on what you saw, your resulting mood would range from suicidal depression to mild happiness.

The mirrors in the rooms of the leprosarium saw scenes that could have been from hell. Every room had a mirror, and from the early morning hours you could hear expletives or howls of pain; proof that Hansen had been busy during the night. Fear drove many to imagine that the lump on their back had grown overnight, that part of their nose had been pushed to the left, or that the skin on the back of their hand had become unnaturally rough. Just imagine what the disease was doing to the back of our eyes: a common headache led to all sorts of thoughts!

So it was that Mycobacterium leprae sculpted away at us, not only bodily but also mentally, sometimes deforming our state of mind in a similar way to the gaping wounds on lepers' backs and shoulders. You could not expect these circumstances to be conducive to the human race's characteristic kindness and optimism, but these traits undeniably existed in the leprosarium too. Perhaps physical ugliness made it easier for that other, more deeply ingrained side of human nature to come out.

I had no cause at all to complain about my room-mate, Robert W. Duncan. He maintained his cheerful nature despite the disease, ignoring its traps and pitfalls. He was also fortunate that the illness progressed very slowly and only drew attention to itself, directed by some inscrutable biological or divine clock, when he thought he was perhaps cured of it.

Robert made my years spent at the leprosarium seem shorter. He never forgot my birthday and he always gave me presents perfectly tailored to my tastes and needs. The most precious of them, the Jugoton pressing of the Beatles' *White Album*, will stay ingrained in my memory forever as the sound of kindness and undiminished friendship. I remember old Ingemar Zoltán listening to 'Back in the USSR' beside the speaker and whooping with joy because he believed it was a propaganda piece, a march conveying an ultimatum to the Soviet tanks in the streets of Budapest. Every day he marched up and down the corridors wanting more, joyfully shouting out a hybridised refrain full of anti-Soviet slogans.

Robert's presents had a mysterious aura of depth and intimacy about them. I would turn them fondly in my hands and had the strange feeling that I had owned them long ago and they had now returned to me, bringing back old memories too. A deck of old Piatnik playing cards, a pocket knife with a rosewood handle, a small ebony-framed Chinese watercolour, a Turkish pipe: each of these gifts had its own special place on my bedside table.

Yet Robert stubbornly refused to say how he came by them, and after badgering him a few times I gave up. It was probably some special ability of his, like a literary or musical talent. Several days before my birthday I followed his movements closely, but Robert was never out of my sight for more than half an hour; not long enough to go to the nearest village or the fertiliser factory. Sometimes he would be walking in the courtyard and cast enigmatic smiles up at me, knowing that I was bursting to ask him one more time: how?

The present he gave me for my forty-second birthday on April 2nd 1989 was kept not on my bedside table but deep inside the woollen filling of the mattress. Robert put it next to the alarm clock so I would see it when the Russian rocket rang hysterically, and when I saw it, my head rang with excitement too. It was a shock that turned the peaceful spring days into a torrent of doubts, assumptions and hopes. What was more, the huge portrait of Nicolae Ceauşescu, which for years had beamed down from the factory administration building opposite, had been smeared beyond recognition with tar.

I shuffled the cards and looked towards the mountains in the west. Beyond the rim of the Transylvanian Alps lay Europe, sinking into another night. I felt it humming like a huge queen bee sending out series of encoded signals. When Robert stole up behind me and tapped me on the shoulder, the cards flew up from my frightened hands and out the window. They fell slowly, it seemed, much too slowly, gliding through the thick spring air. I knew something was about to change.

Robert laughed at my jittery hands. He calmly opened two tins of pineapple rings, one for each of us, and I felt as if he was opening two Pandora's boxes. The next morning you could have seen me walking down the stairs carefully carrying a tin full of water to fetch flowers, those splendid daffodils along the southern wall of the leprosarium.

But that was not the only reason I got up before the others on 16 April 1989.

CHAPTER TWO

It hurt when I swallowed the pineapple, but Robert said that was just a passing phase, after which my oesophagus would become totally numb. That is why lepers in the past often became performers who swallowed live coals or ate glass for money. He said I would get used to it over time, though I would miss the pleasant burning sensation of hot tea. What he missed most of all was the heart-warming burn of the Jim Beam Black he so adored. Robert was American. The only American on the planet infected with this ancient disease, I imagined. He wrote to a few friends and some old aunt in Georgia that he had AIDS and would be spending the rest of his life on the Old Continent. He wanted them to remember him as he had been, as a non-commissioned officer of the US Army, not an enfeebled shadow of his former self. He told me he had picked up leprosy in the brothels of Amsterdam in 1982 and then quickly went on to tell me episodes of his training in Arizona. I did not ask him any more questions, constrained by my good manners, though I knew that none of Hansen's children can explain how they contracted the disease in just one sentence. Their account is extensive and always precisely structured. Lepers talk nineteen to the dozen, at least at a superficial level, whenever they are asked how they arrived at their fate. Robert only told me the whole truth, encouraged by our friendship, after I had been at the leprosarium for many years.

The daffodils were always an unpleasant reminder of the topic of beauty and its reflection. I would not have been surprised if those magnificent flowers suddenly wilted at the sight of my disfigured face. Although I am not missing any vital parts, my nose, cheeks and forehead are covered with large warts, as if peas were growing under the skin. Leontiasis developed, with the result that my eyebrows, eyelashes, hair and beard growth have long since disappeared. But the cartilage of my nose is still in fairly good condition, thanks to regular doses of Thiosemicarbazone and antimony, drugs which were once delivered in abundance. You could do your injections whenever you wanted: before lunch, after breakfast, at dawn or in the middle of the night. The majority of residents adopted a loose regimen like this, not knowing what a double-edged sword it was. Mycobacterium Leprae soon became immune to the medicines so that mammoth doses were needed to stop the progress of the bacillus even for only a short time. With Robert's help, I worked out exactly the right doses of medication to knock out Hansen in the long term. In 1984, the last ampoules of the precious substances ran out. We then switched to therapies with medicinal herbs which we were able to gather in the vicinity of the leprosarium. Several Russian books on herbal medicine helped us quickly work out the most effective infusions for reducing the swelling and painful lumps. Compresses of wild pansy leaves soothed the unbearable itch which came on rainy days and sometimes drove the lepers to claw their already disfigured bodies, producing volcanoes of pus and blood.

Thirty grams of peeled and chopped bittersweet nightshade steeped in a litre of boiling water gave an inconceivably bitter infusion which was good for relieving symptoms in the throat and oesophagus. We gathered the bark of young elm trees all year round in the nearby forest. This was the only plant mentioned in the recipes for alleviating the consequences and symptoms of leprosy, which made it the most popular with the patients. We peeled bark off the stems of two-year-old elms, dried it in an airy place or in the sun, and chopped it up finely. Then we boiled thirteen hundred grams in twenty litres of water until half the liquid had evaporated. Every morning we needed to drink two hundred and fifty millilitres as tea and use the same amount for compresses. We made the infusion in two large cauldrons in the middle of the courtyard and sat around the fire. Old Zoltán had some culinary experience, and his skill in preparing the bark made the work a smooth operation. We would put the speaker on the windowsill and stock the fire well, everyone would bring out a stool or drag up a block of wood, and the fun began. Night after night the White Album revolved, making feet tap in spite of stiff knees. The lepers' dull eyes followed the sparks as they flew up to the heavens.

Robert sometimes took a piece of wood as a microphone and pretended to be performing the magnificent Happiness is a Warm Gun. He enticed sentimental smiles, which our disfigured faces transformed into grotesque portraits of our grief. When our conversation became louder, the music was turned down. Rasping voices would come from under the linen hoods; stories were told of past lives: the vitae of wretches who like witch doctors conjured up lost images and words from the dark limbos of time. No one ever questioned what was said. You could tell your story undisturbed by comments and doubts because everyone knew they would be in a similar situation too.

Whether these biographies were true was not ascertainable. When you arrived at the leprosarium, all documents, personal belongings and clothes were rudely taken off you, and in return you were given a few items of underwear, two white shirts, an army jumper and a quality linen robe with a large hood. New clothes were supplied at regular intervals, so no one could complain about poor hygiene. While three overly amiable doctors accompanied by a Romanian army soldier prepared me for my stay at the leprosarium, I expected they would hang a bell around my neck; an essential accessory of lepers in earlier centuries which warned travellers that one of those deprived of the love of God, was coming along the road. Fortunately that did not happen, but there was something frighteningly decisive about their well-coordinated procedure. I realised that I was not being sent for treatment but being prepared for a different journey to somewhere outside the rules of this world, which could more appropriately be termed 'illness in isolation' than a medical treatment. I wanted to keep my watch, passport and little golden Sagittarius pendant. When I raised this possibility, one of the doctors replied with a gentle sneer, saying that the things would be safer if they were looked after until my treatment was over.

At the same time one of his colleagues threw them into a large metal container while the other, with a mask on his face, rained a white powder over them. Two large needles sank into my thigh, releasing a strong antidepressant and my first dose of Thiosemicarbazone. The doctor dialled zero on the black disk and whispered into the receiver: 'He's ready', then they bundled me into a dilapidated ambulance. I tried to speak, but the injection had silenced my words into gentle arm movements and a wrinkling of my forehead. My tongue rolled lamely in my mouth, making saliva run in strands down my chin and straight on to the floor. I leaned my face against the glass of the back door which had fine wire running through it. The small first-aid station on the outskirts of Bucharest would soon become blurred into a white and red blot on the wall. A man who had not been around during the examination appeared out in front and leant against the wall, waving casually as we left. Wide-lapelled black clothing, a dishevelled jacket, a narrow, neatly shaven moustache above neat rows of teeth: it was this person, whom I later came to know as Mr. Smooth, who had heard the doctor's 'ready' several minutes earlier and with satisfaction lit his cigarette. It hung in his left hand as we left.

As the ambulance rattled along the pockmarked roads on the way to the leprosarium, I sat on the wooden bench at the side, my back against the metal. The wire glass the size of a television screen displayed a pale sfumato of a winter landscape without snow. The villagers in their muddy fields rested their hands on the handles of their tools and watched the ambulance go past. An unnaturally ugly child ran up to the road and threw a stone that clanged against the metal. The driver stopped for a moment and threw back several Romanian swear words. We continued and turned right, into a forest of birch trees and I was lulled to sleep by the monotony of their white trunks bent by the northern wind. As Robert later told me, Mr. Smooth was an officer of the infamous Securitate who had recently been put in charge of all the lepers in the country. He saw to it that they reached their designated destination and, equally important, that they stay there.

The procedure for dealing with leprosy had not changed significantly throughout the several millennia of its known existence. Two simple conditions had to be fulfilled to prevent a drastic spread of the disease: Firstly, lepers' freedom of movement had to be severely restricted; secondly, they had to be prevented from coming into contact with the healthy. It was the same under Ramses II, Charles V or Ivan the Terrible. In the Middle Ages, lepers sometimes made the acquaintance of the stake. Just tell common people about the ungodliness of the contagion and its carriers.

Since the church was not bound by compassion, lepers were forced to establish communities on the peripheries of settlements, seeking their salvation in refuse, medicinal herbs and sour wild fruits. With time, these colonies would become restless and hordes of lepers would plunder nearby villages and rob people travelling to the city. This state of affairs would last several weeks or months depending on the resolve of the city dignitaries to saddle the guard's horses, light torches and go on a small crusade against the sons and daughters of the devil.

The events in Sensotregiore, a city of eight thousand souls one hundred kilometres from Florence, contributed significantly to changing the relationship towards lepers in the sixteenth century. A colony of lepers located just a stone's throw from the city walls had been established in the late fifteenth century at the time of Pope Innocent VIII. The mild and above all dry climate made the area popular with the lepers of southern Europe, and it was not unusual for lepers to arrive from distant parts of Scandinavia, Spain or the British isles. A good supply of herbs, abandoned military stables and a network of roads which allowed gangs of lepers to extort money and food helped the colony grow to a population of two or three thousand by the beginning of the sixteenth century. When a group of colonists brutally raped three under-aged girls (tales speak of them being butchered and eaten at the bacchanalias held that same evening) the city fathers, with the pope's blessing, gathered two hundred heavily armed mercenaries: a force intended to expel this perverted rabble and exact bloody punishment. A battle ensued, and blood-curdling cries were heard until the early hours.

When the curious and vindictive inhabitants of Sensotregiore looked out at the battlefield in the morning light, they were horrified to see a well-ordered army of lepers holding up the heads of their enemies. Now the maddened horde yelled in fury as it converged on the city's fragile gates. Within two hours Sensotregiore had become a Sodom at the mercy of the hungry and disfigured. The humiliated ones now indulged in all the worldly pleasures that had been denied them for years and gave their brutal impulses free rein. A frenzy of rape, plunder, loathsome orgies and cruel murders descended on the city, turning it into a hellhole. The inhabitants, mad with fear of the disease, fled towards the northern gates and out into the hills.

The lepers soon imposed their rule and took over the comfortable homes of the dignitaries. At noon, four members of the city council were hanged on the main square; a mayor was elected, and Sensotregiore became a Lepropolis, a powerful community that functioned well thanks to the financial resources extracted from the hidden niches, mattresses and safes located in the houses of the rich. Naturally, no army existed that was prepared to attack a city in which leprosy reigned, but leper colonies throughout Europe were punished in revenge for Sensotregiore. Their wooden huts were burned down without mercy, and every soldier had tacit permission to kill or spare lepers as he saw fit. Not until a decade after the establishment of Lepropolis, by which time over two thirds of its inhabitants had succumbed to the disease, did this change: a host of three hundred cavalrymen and an equal number of well-armed infantry arrived at the city gates determined to put an end to Sodom and restore divine order. Among the soldiers were many former inhabitants of Sensotregiore imbued with righteous rage and a burning hatred. Alerted by the fanfares and the rattle of weapons, the lepers left the city without a fight and made off into the mountains with the sabres of the victors close behind them.

This was Robert's favourite tale, and he was often requested by the others to tell it as we sat around the fireside After a final dramatic pause, he never failed to mention that if you passed by the half-ruined citadel of that small Italian city today you could still hear the cries of our profligate brothers who had fallen into sin.

The doctor shook me awake when we arrived at the gate of the leprosarium. I was given a personal hygiene kit and the driver offered me a cigarette. If I had accepted, I suppose he would have flicked it to me through the gap of the slightly opened window. Old Zoltán and Robert W. Duncan waited on the other side of the fence and were the first people in several months to offer me their hands. We strode through thick layers of fallen leaves and stepped around frozen puddles. The leprosarium was a three-storey building with high ceilings. I saw dark silhouettes standing at several dimly lit windows. The third storey had small ventilation openings only and was used for storage.

The room was well heated, and several loads of finely chopped firewood lay stacked by the stone stove in the corner. There were flowers on the bedside table, a reproduction of the Raft of the Medusa above the bed and a crucifix at the head of the bed. Robert was visibly gladdened by my good English and chattered happily as he showed me around the building that was to be my only home for years to come. After pointing out the location of the bathroom, he left me to unpack. Dinner was at eight thirty and the dining room was on the ground floor. I looked out the window and tried to catch a glimpse of the surroundings through the darkness, but all I saw were the flickering violet lights of the nearby fertiliser factory.

The corridors of the building were curved like crescents. Standing in the middle of a floor you couldn't see either of the ends. This confused me at first, and I often went the wrong way and ended up at the locked door of the stairway that led up to the attic.

My first look into the dining room revealed a round table of enormous size set with simple plates and cutlery; patients in their dark-hooded robes sat at their places. When I entered I heard a friendly murmur of different languages and dialects, but no one stood up to greet me. Old Zoltán pointed to a vacant chair next to his, and at the same time Robert began introducing the other patients with whom I would 'share the good and the bad', as he put it. When their names were called out, each answered by pulling back his hood. One after another they emerged; heads crafted by leprosy, skulls covered with varying textures of scarred and malformed tissue. Monsters they were, but they spoke with human voices, which created the impression that they were people wearing ghastly masks. Then I threw back my hood too.

I cannot claim to have had anything like rosy cheeks any more, but my skin was still fairly smooth with only a few rough patches caused by the beginnings of leprosy. The tendons on my neck trembled, a sign of recent health, and my hair had only just begun to fall out. All this provoked a minute of hushed envy and disbelief. Robert broke the silence by reaching for the oval dish of boiled vegetables and giving me a big helping.

We pulled our hoods back over our heads and the eating continued. The rest of the meal was seasoned with barely audible whispers further muffled by the linen hoods. The others served me food too, without missing the opportunity to look me in the eyes and inspect my hands, searching for explicit signs of the disease. They saw the beginnings of lumpy excrescences on the joints of my fingers as well as my veil-like cataract; they saw shining tears of desperation that dried and disappeared before they could roll. But my mood gradually improved and it seemed I was accepted as a fully-fledged member of the community.

Later, back in the room, Robert tried to dispel the fear generated by my first major encounter with the disease. Leprosy did not have to progress any further than it already had, he explained; we would take a regular course of Thiosemicarbazone and do all we could to lessen the effects. I did not share his optimism. One more visual encounter with the other patients at breakfast forced me to realise what an uncompromising monster dwelt within me.

I watched their faces as they chewed their fried eggs. Lumps of dead flesh shook like jelly and shone like grease. Their mutilated fingers looked like lumps of melted lead, and their sunken eyes cast reflections of the faint light that barely reached them. Some of them would interrupt their meal for a moment to remove pieces of food from their open sinuses, which elicited loud complaints from the others, so the poor noseless fellows would have to get up from the table and finish their dirty work out of sight.

The oldest denizen of Europe's last leprosarium was Zoltán, who had lived there since it was founded in 1928. He was the only one to survive the German occupation and mass execution when forty-seven residents were taken out into a field and mowed down into a muddy pit.

He remembered the noise of the armoured vehicles on 14 December 1942, the iron gate being broken down, and the young soldiers of the 'Prinz Eugen' division determined to... Oh God, and were they determined! Four young soldiers in protective suits ran up and down the corridors, waking the residents and ordering them to stretch their legs and go out to the courtyard immediately. They came out one after another, rubbing their eyes. The arrival of the Germans did not provoke any great panic, Zoltán explained. The residents were more surprised than anything else because at that stage they did not quite know what was going on in the world outside. They assumed this was just another of the humiliating head-counts that the authorities conducted for fear of the patients fleeing and causing an epidemic. In fact, the German soldiers armed to the teeth standing in the courtyard were a reason to hope for the introduction of order and proper medical care to alleviate the desperate conditions at the colony. But when the officer in charge pointed towards the gate with his Schmeisser and the first in the line of lepers was jabbed in the ribs with it and told to move, Zoltán realised that something other than ordinary medical treatment or boring head-counting was in store for them. The minute of machine-gun fire confirmed his doubts. Curled up under the two-year old elm trees close to the fence, Zoltán cried big, cold tears that dripped to the ground. He wanted to pass away like his brothers, to nestle against their bodies and end this miserable lazar's life in the backwoods of Romania.

The Germans carried out a thorough disinfection of the building by burning everything flammable out in the courtyard. Several valuable portraits of Queen Marie of Romania were destroyed in the flames together with the pieces of expensive walnut-wood furniture; they and the pictures had been given to the leprosarium as presents of the crown. Zoltán watched as the blaze swallowed up painstakingly preserved mementoes. Photographs of friends and family as well as small but cherished items kept in drawers near the patients' bed heads all vanished amidst the red tongues of the Germans' fire.

That morning, Zoltán told us, his last hopes went up in smoke. Be it this country or the lands beyond the mountains that hummed like a fat queen bee sending out encoded signals; never would this world become a place worthy of God's love.

Zoltán roamed the nearby forests until the end of the war; he slept in abandoned stables and burned-down houses. The Germans created a well-guarded headquarters in the leprosarium building, and the courtyard was patrolled not only by guards but also three bloodthirsty Alsatians. Zoltán did not dare to take a closer look.

On 17 April 1944, dawn found him in the stench of a chicken coop close to the main road. He was woken by that same humming of mighty machines and the incisive sounds of German. He waited for the soldiers to pass and then headed for the leprosarium with quickening steps. Now in the courtyard a mighty blaze was devouring the belongings of the German soldiers: countless bundles of documents, epaulettes of various ranks, and large photographs of Adolf Hitler. Yet the building remained untouched. Apart from a large swastika crudely daubed in tar on the front wall before the Nazis' withdrawal, there were no visible signs of destruction. On the contrary, the windows had been repaired, the bathrooms sanitised, and every room now had a small stone stove. Solid, functional furniture adorned the dining room which was polished to splendour, and in the kitchen the aromas of the last meal still hung in the air. Crockery bearing the mark of the Reich shone in the china closets. Zoltán touched it with his crooked fingers and looked at his reflection on the white porcelain surfaces.

In the corner of the dining room he spotted the bulging copper horn of a gramophone. He picked up one of records which lay scattered on the floor, wound up the spring and gently placed the stylus between the black grooves of Grieg's Piano Concerto. The music resounded as he donned the last remaining overcoat that hung in the corridor and tore the epaulettes and the Iron Cross from the breast. *Allegro molto moderato*: Zoltán goes outside to the southern wall to see if there are still any of the daffodils that usually grow there at this time of year. *Adagio*: Zoltán picks daffodils, angrily tearing them out of the ground. His cold tears drip on the resilient petals. Allegro molte e marcato: he slowly lays the flowers on the round depression in the ground not far from the leprosarium. *Aase's Death*: he lays himself on the warm spring earth, on the bodies of his leprous brothers that have turned to dust.

Ants feasted on the filth and sweat of Zoltán's unwashed body, carrying away those tasty morsels to the tiny passages of their subterranean home. After he had slept for several hours, he went and had a bath, bandaged his wounds with fresh bandages and went back to the resting place of his friends. Instead of saying a prayer, above their grave he read out the fifth chapter of the Second Book of Kings, in which Elisha heals the leper Naaman of Syria and punishes Gehazi by giving him leprosy. It's not hard to imagine who Zoltán had in mind when he spoke those Old Testament curses.

If you asked him why he decided to spend the rest of his life at the leprosarium, he would wave dismissively and say with resignation, 'I'm waiting for Death to come. This is the only place I can wait undisturbed.'

A commemorative lunch was held every 14 December to mark the death of our former fellow-sufferers; a minute's silence was observed and a joint prayer spoken at the mass grave. After telling the story for the umpteenth time, Zoltán would wipe away his tears with his thumb, the only healthy finger of his right hand, and go off to bed. We broke up in silence, moved and somehow proud that lepers had played a part in the Second World War, albeit through collective execution.

If Zoltán had cast off his documentarian chains for a moment and given his imagination free rein, he might have been able to spin a story about how, cowering under the elms, he had heard the defiant shouts of those prepared to die; he might have said that they started singing the 'Internationale' in unison in different languages until this was cut short by a burst of fire in the middle of the second stanza, for example. Since he was the sole survivor, and the post-war Communist authorities were eager to present myths of heroism, they would have embraced his far-fetched tale with open arms. A charming memorial centre would have been built nearby and the leprosarium would have been given central heating.

As my coarse hands descended among the heads of the daffodils, I looked around me to make sure I was the only leper awake that morning. I snapped the young stems and put the flowers in the cold water of the pineapple tin. The birthday present Robert had given me was hidden in my inside pocket. Seven daffodils: the seventh stone from the left in the sixth row from the bottom. I prodded with a piece of wood and dislodged the stone so I could get a grip on it and pull it out. Robert advised me to 'push in steadily' and 'pull back slowly'. The stone creaked like an old mill wheel, I thought, though I had never been in a mill. It was heavier than I imagined. Putting the stone down by my legs, I rolled up my right sleeve as far as it would go, and reached my hand timidly into the dark hole. I breathed in the cold of the old wall and expected something to touch me, but I did not feel anything. There was just the cold and the smell of moss. I took the present out of my pocket, laid it in the dark hole and then pushed the stone block in hard. Then I carefully picked up the tin and went back to the room. I was excited; I felt as if I had just planted a magic seed in the wall and wondered what kind of strange fruit would spring forth.

CHAPTER THREE

Robert spent the hours of afternoon resting up in the room if it was not necessary to pick elm bark or chop firewood. He sat on the bed with his back against the wall, from where he could see the tops of the trees beyond the fence and Ceauşescu's forced smile on the factory wall. He took a book down off the shelf, one of the senseless works in his improvised personal library, and leafed through it at length until the dictator's face was bathed in the ruddy light of the early-evening sun. He would stop at particular pages, and the silence was interrupted by facts and figures: the population of Romania in 1903, the amount of aluminium exported to the East Bloc countries or the growth rates of national income in the 1970s. Robert had found all these books at the factory's rubbish dump which he and the others visited two or three times a year when the workers, due to some national holiday, only worked one shift. The thick volumes from the National Statistics Office had lain among the rusty remains of furniture corroded by ammonia.

Rummaging through the rubbish involved a certain risk because any particles of chemical fertiliser that came into contact with leprous lesions caused pain and bleeding which lasted for days. Hands and feet had to be well protected and a moist cloth worn over the nose. They found cups with broken handles, ornamental plates with the old Romanian coat of arms, worn-out tools which they later sold to one another for several equally worthless Romanian lei made of aluminium or copper. The copy of the Bible in Russian which had strayed in amongst the statistics books was precious to Robert. He read it from cover to cover with interest, refreshing his knowledge of Russian. When he became immersed in one of his books and moved it closer to his furrowed face or licked his fingers so he could turn the pages more easily, a whistling came from his head, first quietly, but becoming progressively louder. Then I knew he was walking the broad asphalt and asbestos roads, looking at the luxuriant maples of his native Gainesville and thinking of Georgia. *'I am a poor wayfaring stranger / Travelling through this world of woe,'* he whistled. He did not need to purse his lips to produce the melody. Robert's nose was deformed in such a way that his left nostril, which was very narrow and swollen inside, created a pleasant, uniform whistle when he exhaled evenly, and he put this to good use. By adjusting his upper lip he could almost produce the whole scale, and he often liked to say that an organ had grown in his head. He whistled, *'Yet there's no sickness, toil or danger / In that bright land to which I go. / I'm only going over Jordan / I'm only going over home.'*

He was thinking of his native country which he last saw long ago, in 1969, when he was an NCO and intelligence officer in the US Army on his way to Berlin. Actually he only saw clouds through the thick glass porthole as the four-engined Hercules cruised over the plains of Texas, Oklahoma and Missouri; later the snowy peaks of the Appalachians appeared. He wanted to be alert and not let sleep lean his head against the metal insides of the plane, he wanted to be awake when they flew over the Statue of Liberty. In those days, planes took off from military airports in the west of the country to cross the Atlantic to bases in Germany and Italy, from where they continued on to Vietnam; all of them descending low enough for the soldiers to say farewell to the girl with the torch and strike up The Star-Spangled Banner. Seeing the Statue of Liberty was a superstitious obligation: it brought the good luck one needed. But Robert was stretched out as comfortably as possible, laced up in his uniform and hemmed in by his two neighbours, and only woke up when the lights of the United Kingdom were beneath them. Just two more hours to Berlin and his spick-and-span boots would be treading the soil of Europe; they would march the Old Continent guided by clear orders and an even clearer will to be a good, dutiful soldier.

Sitting on his bed and staring at the crowns of the trees beyond the leprosarium fence, Robert spoke at length about what he felt when he first set foot on the land of his distant ancestors. The first thing he felt was unbearable pain as he jumped exuberantly from the middle step of the gangway, lost his balance and crashed into the wooden support structure. A board broke and a large splinter stabbed through the thick leather of his boot and deep into his sole. He saw sparks. Cold sweat trickled from his armpits as he rushed to return to the marching rhythm of his guard unit, not wanting anyone to notice his little accident. He marched with a firm step, and all the time a lake of blood squelched beneath his heel. He looked into the sky over Berlin. The red lights of military planes emerged from the low clouds and Robert imagined they were drops of his own blood that had merged with the rain and were beginning to fall on German soil. He told me that this painful first acquaintance with Europe somehow set his general mood for the years that followed. Whenever he went down an orderly Berlin staircase or the last steps of an underground station, his left foot would faintly twitch; a deep and painful tremble reminding him where he was.

It was much to his liking, therefore, that he did not have to wear boots for a long time after the accident. Instead he wore the most comfortable of shoes: classic Dr Scholls to match his civilian suit and light raincoat. They belonged to his new task of uncovering a Russian intelligence network, which at that time, – the late sixties and early seventies, – was very effective at uncovering all kinds of information on the location and activities of American troops. Apart from Nikolai Vladimirovich Sigidin, whose Russian accent allowed him to play peasant roles in Russian dramas at small West Berlin theatres, Robert did not meet one single Russian in a whole year. That was a sign of their skill, he supposed. He tried to grasp what he was actually searching for, but he did not dare to ask more than he was told at the monthly briefings in the basement office at the military airport. He thought asking questions would only make him seem suspicious, so he nodded intently as he wrote down the bars and restaurants he should visit to listen for whispers in Russian. Besides, he did not want to lose his comfortable accommodation in Hotel August, Fasanenstrasse no. 22, nor the fifteen hundred dollars monthly, of which he only converted half into deutschmarks. The rest was put aside for quiet times to come in Georgia; a large black Buick, a good motor boat and Mitchell fishing gear.

His days in Berlin began with an excellent hotel breakfast followed by morning coffee in Café Berio not far from Winterfeldtplatz. Midday laziness led him back towards the hotel; to the quiet, extensive record shops where he supplemented his private collection of works by well-known and more obscure European composers. At lunchtime he would look through the finely printed texts on the record covers and afterwards retire to his room for an hour's nap to the sounds of his Phillips gramophone. The afternoons brought more duties: Russian lessons, an hour of grammar and another of conversation, lonely wandering through the twilight streets, basement night clubs and a few beers.

He would remember the spring of 1969 for the long walks with Martha Goldberg and her loud laughter at Berlin's acoustic underground stations. He did not know why, but her laugh often reminded him of Brahms's Hungarian Dance Number 6.

The mornings became bright and full of fragrance. He replaced his suit with a smart velvet jacket and bought carnations from the street seller. In those days he often reflected on that simple kind of beauty which roused in him hen Martha's silhouette came gliding along the pavement, growing steadily larger and larger; or when the lady grocer, a real Brunhilde, wrapped up a lettuce and held it out to him in her healthy, red hands at her sunlit stall. Things would have been perfect had it not been for the notification from his operations centre unceremoniously thrust under his hotel-room door. All briefings were cancelled, it said, 'until further notice'; intelligence officers had to be especially careful 'while out on assignment' as there were indications that Russian agents had become increasingly active and 'did not hesitate to employ brutal methods' to acquire valuable information. A footnote typed in italics added that all staff, given the heightened risk entailed in their work, would receive double pay for as long as this Third-Degree State of Alert was in force. The operations centre also mentioned in a footnote to the footnote that agents who were captured by hostile intelligence services, with or without regard to culpability, would be considered non-existent. In other words, US intelligence would deny that they lived and breathed and would take no steps to liberate or defend them.

Robert had been acquainted with rules and vocabulary of this kind during his training in Arizona. They were strange manoeuvres of language in uniform, he thought, but they greatly facilitated communication between people in his line of work.

While carrying a bouquet of nine flowers, Robert W. Duncan felt a dull blow to the back of his head and a wave of tiredness washed over him. The carnations spilled over the pavement. He saw a grey veil spangled with thousands of sparks, and then nothing. He dreamed of pigs, a herd of dirty pigs, running round and round in circles and baring their teeth. His body remembered a long journey through Berlin's streets, and the pain in his ribs when he awoke announced that more blows were to come.

Eventually, his eyelids began to glow with a blinding pink. It heralded light, a lot of light, but Robert hesitated to open his eyes fully. When he rolled his gaze briefly in the hope of seeing a sandy beach and beautiful clear water amidst that intense glare, a bucketful of cold water slapped his face. He heard the water still dripping and the bucket being put down on the floor, and then several harsh words demanding that he wake up. He was in a well-lit room without windows, sitting with loosely bound hands on a wooden stool. A column of smoke rose in the corner to his left. The smoke began to move from left to right with a gentle stamping of shoes. He saw shoes, brown pants, the shining buckle of a belt, a shirt with the sleeves rolled up and a large head with a Mickey Mouse mask. When the person wanted to draw from the cigarette he would hold it with two fingers and stick it into the small opening of the mask's mouth, and when he exhaled white wisps went off in all directions creating a mane around the frozen features of the face. Mickey Mouse started asking questions. When, how, where? How many, where to, what for? Names, names, names. Water dripped from Robert's nose and he tried to catch the drops with the tip of his tongue. He told the interrogator everything he knew: just a few sentences with very basic operative details. He swallowed and shrugged his shoulders, realising there was nothing more to tell, and his vocal cords released a hysterical laugh. The questions were replaced by blows, the blows interrupted by his unnatural giggling, and finally silenced by a large injection of barbiturates. Mickey Mouse melted into the darkness, and as Robert struggled to maintain the last vestiges of consciousness he felt he was sitting in an aeroplane. The Statue of Liberty was beckoning to him with her blazing torch: she came running across the ocean with great strides and she had something to tell him. But soon darkness fell on those images too.

This time he did not wake up with a glowing pink in his eyes; he saw a moist brown mist in which he imagined blurred silhouettes of hairy, bearded men. A heavy smell of human excrement entered his nostrils and filled his lungs with a sickly sweet odour. His hands were free. As he rubbed his swollen face it hurt. His right cheekbone was covered in a painful blister, and when he tried to straighten his back something ran up his spine like the bites of a thousand red ants. Cascades of cold air flooded in through a window with rusty bars high up in the wall. His knees trembled from the cold. Back under the Arizona sun he had thought about the possible risks of his work, but all he was able to imagine were the damp cobbled streets of Berlin filled with the intermittent rattle of trams and roamed by the tall figures of well-groomed Russian and East German agents. He was moved by the thought that he would become part of that scene. He wanted to be in Europe: a patchwork of different languages divided by well-guarded borders, the Old Continent, saturated with blood and history. His expectations coincided with the exotic stereotype that every American dreams of visiting their ancestral home at least once in their life. He enjoyed that feeling.

The foul-smelling cell was worse than anything Robert could have imagined. He had wanted to be in Europe, and now here he was. As his eyes became accustomed to the dark he saw roughly lain bricks beyond the bars on the window, which suggested he was again in a cellar. He felt something moving up his throat, his stomach tightened and his breathing became rapid. He began to cry.

He was woken from his sleep by a rectangular frame of light, highlighting the outlines of a doorway. He had thought the door was on the opposite side, so he was not sure whether he just imagined the light or whether he really saw it, yet he saw the dimensions of the cell more clearly now. All of a sudden a rattling cough came from the right, from beneath a pile of filthy blankets. At one end a foot stuck out, almost black, at the other end he saw greasy locks of hair and an arm lying alongside the body. The upper arm was covered in large, bulging blisters that exuded pus and blood. The flesh was decaying.

Robert crawled on his knees to the decomposing corpse. He looked for a face among the locks of hair but found only hardened bulges ready to turn into ghastly lesions. He pulled back the soiled blankets. The unbearable smell of a body rotting, of a corpse giving up the last signs of life, made him sick. He did not have the strength to even bang on the door; he was so frightened. It seemed the enemy was shamelessly betraying the rules of the game. He felt he was sinking into unconsciousness again, and at the same time he hoped he would wake up somewhere else. Let it be anywhere, he thought, even somewhere more terrible, but not here in this grave.

He was brought back to consciousness by the furtive turning of a key in a rusty lock. And then came the light: a flood of light which revealed that there was no one else in the cell except for him and the zombie under the blankets. The silhouettes of hairy men were actually large sacks filled with soil. They could kill him here, cut off his limbs and chop the torso in half. The pieces could be put in five or six sacks and buried in just as many separate graves. He decided he had to get through the door and began to crawl. His knees stung unbearably. His dried-out face, misshapen by the blows, crackled like a dry leaf whenever he grimaced in pain. He made it through the door, but before he could even raise his head he was welcomed by a black army boot in his ribs, forceful and fast. Another kick came from the other side. The door slammed behind his back. He was glad to hear that sound; he would not have to go back into the cell now, he imagined. Two shaven heads towered above him, men in light-green uniforms without insignia. Their faces revealed indifference and a cynical satisfaction with Robert's situation.

As Robert sat cross-legged on the bed and told me about his misfortunes in Berlin, he absently turned the pages of the Bible. Sometimes I even imagined he was reading everything out of the book. His fingers left traces of sweat on the transparent biblical paper. His words left a host of mysteries about his tale but I didn't dare to ask any questions. Not with the tears brimming on Robert's eyelids, not when a page of the Third Book of Moses was torn out in fury (he was to stick it in again neatly the next day).

Yet at that spot, just when the holy words were torn out of their millennia-old order, my friend added something to the story that lay aborted on the floor of an unknown Berlin cellar. Strong arms grabbed him and dragged him down a long corridor, at the end of which another door opened. His legs struck against steps going up, and his heart pounded at the thought that this journey might soon come to an end. At the top of the stairs he was splashed with fresh spring air, which made his head spin. He saw a new moon hanging low above the nearby buildings in which no light shone. He had no idea where he was. Then there was another dull blow to the back of his head.

They threw him out onto the same pavement. Maybe at exactly the same spot where the bouquet of carnations he was taking to Martha Goldberg had spilled. There was a public telephone at the bus stop about one hundred metres away. Several people were waiting and Robert hoped he would be able to get some coins from them for the phone. As he approached they all drew back. An old man hastily inserted a few coins and let him dial. The telephone swallowed the metal, and a familiar voice at the other end informed Robert icily that he would be picked up in twenty minutes. He wanted to thank the old man, but he only raised his stick and yelled: 'Get back!'

Robert sat on the bench fingering his sores and bruises. Only now did he begin to realise what had actually happened. He knew that his career as a well-paid intelligence officer in the US Army was over, because he was not allowed to talk. However insignificant it seemed, the information he knew (and which 'They' now knew) was the very heart of the work, the essence of the secret. It had to be protected at all costs. He had expected a black Mercedes to come and take him to the dispensary and hospital at the airport, but instead it was a yellow VW van that came, with darkened windows and advertising for detergent. The back door opened. A man in overalls waved for him to get in. A coarse army blanket lay on the metal floor. The door slammed. Robert recalled the Mickey Mouse mask and its frozen smile that conveyed a grotesque and paralysing dread. He regretted that his last journey through Berlin's streets was in a metal box. Through the small, barred pane of glass he only saw the heads that swayed as the van turned bends. They arrived at the airport even quicker than he had hoped. And then: the calm, regular footfall of military boots, a stretcher, a smiling doctor and a serious nurse, rubber gloves taking his pulse. Plain, no-nonsense procedure, he thought.

The strength of the American military machine lay in its strict observance of procedure, so Robert had to go through a whole series of measures prescribed for cases such as this. Rigorous medical examinations were followed by a long interrogation which went into the most minuscule of details. Was there any writing on the walls of the cell where you were held? How tall was the interrogator? Did he have an accent? Do you remember any scar on his neck or hands? Were the blows delivered with the fists or some object? What brand of cigarettes did he smoke? Did you see the packet? Did you talk with the other person confined in the cell? How many bars were there on the windows? How many sacks of soil?

Robert was afraid of the questions. Lying in the sterile dark of the hospital room he tried to phrase his answers in advance. The noise of the planes shook the glass, and when the four-engined Hercules landed he felt the shudder in his chest.

He did not get out of bed that first night. After a good meal and two cans of Coca-Cola he entertained himself by burping and counting the white tiles on the walls. He expected he would be woken at dawn by amiable uniformed personnel and taken to a compartment of the office, where they would write down everything he said. But Robert did not wait for them to wake him. He got up at first light, donned the hospital dressing gown, combed his hair and sat on the bed to watch the door. After an hour he began to walk up and down, counting the tiles on the floor. The doorknob was immobile, impassive. Music came from the corridor. The announcer of the armed forces' radio station gave the exact time at half-hourly intervals. It was the programme with soldiers' music requests and news from the 'Eastern Front'. Robert wondered if Berlin was perhaps considered a Western battlefield, where a different kind of war was taking place. Finally a sign: steps coming towards the door, the radio went silent, remained silent for several minutes, and then went on again louder than before. The sound of steps again. The latch would creak any moment now, he imagined, telling himself that the radio must have been turned off to allow the doctor some peace during his morning rounds. Robert's room was the last, at the end of the corridor, so a slight delay could be forgiven. He peered into the keyhole, and sweat covered his hands. He heard the scrape of a key in the lock.

Only now did Robert realise that he was being held under a kind of temporary arrest; the shadow of the soldier he had seen through the slats of the venetian blind patrolling every ten minutes during the night had been there because of him. When he heard the screech of the ungreased metal, he decided not to ask why he was being held under lock and key, under guard. He told himself it was all part of the normal procedure. After the interrogation, and the filing of a precise report, everything would be alright, Robert thought. He would be given half a year's pay in advance and returned to Arizona the next day on the first flight. Or maybe he would be allowed to land at the airport in New York. After several days in the Big Apple spending money he would head back to Gainesville, Georgia. But another surprise was in store for him.

Instead of a smiling doctor and serious nurse, three people entered the room in protective suits and the kind of gas masks Robert had once seen during ABC protection exercises. One was carrying a tray with a large schnitzel, tomato salad and mushroom sauce; a second tray was laden with bottles of medicines and several glass syringes filled with a bluish liquid. The third frogman was not carrying anything. He took the chair, placed it by the bed and sat down. Large beads of sweat appeared on Robert's forehead above his panic-filled face, full of questions. In the frogman's visor Robert saw a tiny figure with bowed shoulders that nervously clenched the edge of the bed sheet. It was himself that he saw as he tried to discern some human expression, a mouth and a nose, behind the glass. A muffled voice that sounded like it came from out of a plastic pit asked one of the tray-bearing colleagues to go out and turn off the radio. They interrupted Wayfaring Stranger in the third strophe: *'Yet beauteous fields lie just before me / Where God's redeemed their...'*. Cut. Deafening silence filled with the artificial sound of breathing through filters. The voice spoke again: 'Mr Duncan, we have reason to believe that your health... I mean... There are indications that your health is in grave danger.' Robert nodded to indicate he understood. A large drop of sweat flew from his nose and landed on his hand. The frogman continued: 'I don't want to call the situation extremely serious, but I would say it is in your interest – and in the interest of all of us – for you to spend several more days in quarantine for further tests. I'm sure you understand.' Robert said nothing. He rolled up his sleeve submissively when the needle approached his upper arm. He could not speak. His whole body shook. He felt a cold wave race through him and, several seconds later, a steady humming in his head from the potent injection. They advised him to lie down and have a good rest. And not to worry: after all, he was on safe ground. They were aware of the pain and torment he had been through, they said, but he had to hold on for a little longer. Robert wondered what 'a little longer' meant; he did not suspect that it would mean years, decades of his life in the dark hinterland of Europe. He stared at the ceiling and waited for the impulse to do something sensible: to scream with fear and to fight at the edge of this ominous abyss. At this moment his present life, and all that was to come, had become a little black clot caught up in the unpredictable bloodstream of fate.

After he had eaten they tried hard to convince him that he was still healthy. When he asked how many months and days he had left, one of the frogmen shook with unnatural laughter. Robert made out fine lips and big blue eyes behind the glass visor. They asked him about people he had met, about their hands, the colour of their skin and the appearance of their faces, and when Robert came to the part about the foul-smelling basement cell and the body covered in blankets, the doctor slapped his leg so his colleague would begin taking notes. Skin colour, lesions, the condition of limbs and face, hair, smells, any coughing? They wrote down all the details Robert remembered, nodding eagerly. One more injection was given and a sample of mucous membrane taken from Robert's nose.

The doctor brought Robert his dinner in person, offered him a cigarette and this time sat at the foot of the bed. 'The incubation period can last for years,' he said. 'The rules state that you can't go home before you're cured, so as not to endanger American citizens,' was the next piece of information. 'The internal regulations say you can't stay at the base,' he told Robert. 'The army will cover the costs of your treatment.' The doctor filled in the gaps between these statements with talk of global climatic changes, of the woman who was waiting for him in Seattle and could not go on waiting alone, of cold meals out in the field, all of which was accompanied by the vacuous melodies of the armed forces' radio station. 'Europe's last leprosarium is in south-eastern Romania,' he added.

CHAPTER FOUR

The morning I hid my birthday present, a Romanian passport wrapped in wax paper, then put the tin of daffodils down on the windowsill slowly and quietly so as not to wake Robert who lay facing the wall – that morning was the first time I thought about escaping. The plume of smoke from the factory curled above the plain like a giant question mark until the wind and strong spring sun turned it to a grey river that flowed away to the west.

Robert was talking in his sleep. He pressed his face into the pillow, and when he turned over he left bright spots of blood. It's a known fact that almost all lepers are plagued by insomnia, even in the early stages of the disease. No position is comfortable for the afflicted body. I think we would only find peace if we could sleep standing up, like sleepwalkers. On pleasant days a few of us would always be sitting on the edge of the old fountain in the leprosarium's courtyard, exhausted by lack of sleep. We would bask in the spring sunshine and levitate on the border of consciousness. Such problems were foreign to Robert, who was now sleeping soundly and snoring like an elephant.

I drew a chair up to the window. From there I could see the spot in the wall where the birthday present from Robert was hidden. I had the feeling that the outlines of the stone were clearly visible and that it was moving all by itself. I feared it would fall out at any minute and the passport would flutter off into the sky like a black bird. My friend stretched and made extended waking-up noises. He leaned against the wall and told me that Paul McCartney had killed John Lennon with one slash of a knife. He laughed and drew his index finger across his throat. 'Can't buy me love', he said, and went on humming the melody.

The first page of the passport was taken up by the photograph which the Romanian soldier took in the tiny first-aid station when I was being prepared for the leprosarium. My new name was Andrei Stanescu; beneath it was an ID number, the Romanian coat of arms and the signature of an authorised official in Bucharest. The face showed no signs of the disease, but the black and white photo radiated fear and confusion, and there was a strange shine in the pupils which were looking away to the side. Back then I still bore the stamp of that other world, of years of a relatively peaceful life which were slowly sinking into the quicksand of oblivion, entering the swamps of the future.

Whenever I recalled the cities of my childhood, muttered vulgarisms in my mother tongue or looked at the dirty map of Europe dredged up from the fertiliser factory's rubbish dump, I felt a pang of nostalgia that brought tears to my eyes. Wisps of colour, traces of familiar odours and voices, voices, voices. But in the last few years, memories of this kind aroused less and less emotion. They seemed too far away to pompously step onto my mind's stage and put on their show. They simply hung around in my thoughts like the last herd of three dozen bison in the forests of northern Poland: you only saw them if you looked for them. A strong wire fence protects them; one after another they disappear into the mud, worthless heaps of sinewy meat. They are dying out.

Yet the passport had forced me to rethink everything. When I opened it I felt I was leafing through a thick notebook full of fine print and not twenty empty pages of official blue.

I sat down on my bed. Robert got up, wished me a good morning and sat on the chair by the window. Zoltán was milling around in the courtyard and muttering under his breath. Robert waved to him, and he replied grumpily with the three stiff fingers of his left hand. He had large red blotches on his forehead and scalp which made the hairless skin, furrowed by leprosy, look like the relief map of some forgotten continent.

I waited for Robert to mention the passport and ask if I had hidden it, but he just sat there quietly with his elbows propped on the windowsill and watched Zoltán walking in circles on the dry ground around the fountain. He smelt the daffodils and stroked the petals with the tips of his fingers. Suddenly he put his hand to his right ear and with his other hand made a sign that I should be quiet. He was trying to concentrate on a sound which my sense of hearing had not yet detected. 'Can you hear it?' he asked me, putting his finger to his lips again. For a few moments I could not distinguish anything except the constant murmur of the trees and the increasingly frequent scrape of Zoltán's steps.

Like the sound of a distant aeroplane coming closer and closer to the runway, the air began to tremble, filled with hundreds of voices. There was singing, the rousing melody of the 'Internationale' mixed with workers' chanting in Romanian, in which I recognised slogans like, 'Down with the dictator!', Freedom!', 'We want our rights!', 'Equality!' Zoltán stopped his pacing and shambled to the fence as fast as his body would carry him. From our window we made out banners attached to long poles, Romanian tricolour flags with a hole where the state emblem used to be and a river of blue overalls which cast up a cloud of dust. Several farmers who were out in the fields joined the column together with two loud tractors; dozens of protestors climbed up onto them like ants. This improvised army now headed for the fortress that was the factory. It was all like a modern adaptation of Robert's tale about Sensotregiore and the bloody battle beneath its walls.

The whole demonstration stopped for a moment to cheer the reporter's car that arrived from the Romanian national television station, though it parked at a safe distance. The cameraman climbed up onto the roof of the beat-up vehicle and from there filmed the events that were to follow.

The leprosarium came alive too. Everyone gathered around the second-floor windows to get a better view of things. The road to the factory wound past fields of corn, through a birch wood, traced a broad semicircle around some power-line poles, coming within a few hundred metres of the leprosarium fence, and then turned away again towards the factory, passing the rubbish dump on the way. On top of the large storehouse several police helmets shone; an officer pointed with his truncheon and deployed policemen armed with rifles at the corners.

Zoltán held on to the fence and jumped up and down. He cursed Ceauşescu and joined in the hubbub, singing several verses of the 'Internationale'. As the blue river came closer to the leprosarium, Zoltán's cries became louder and more excited. When the workers were at the closest point to the leprosarium and Robert's eagle eyes could make out their dirty, unshaven faces, we all watched as Zoltán jumped the fence, tripped over the wire, then straightened his linen robe, pulled on his hood and strode towards the workers with open arms to join in their chanting and singing. When the crowd came close to him it went a little quieter. Curious eyes stared at our castle of contagion, a house of the accursed that shimmered like a mirage among all their social problems.

They saw Zoltán, and absolute silence fell. But the old man was not put off by the mass of gaping eyes, nor the ill-tempered agitation and ever more frequent cries. He was convinced of the friendly disposition of the tormented people who were rising up against the tyrant.

The first stone flew from the midst of the crowd and fell several metres in front of Zoltán. Robert and I had already jumped the fence and were hastening towards him; while he happily waved his arms and droned the same song. He still did not want to believe that the 'prisoners of starvation and wretched of the earth' needed no leprous ally wrapped in linen rags; that for them he was an abomination from another world. More stones whistled through the air. At first subdued, then louder and louder, there came shouts of, 'Unclean! Unclean!' I was stunned to hear this ancient cry, now directed at us, as we grabbed Zoltán by the arms and dragged him back. Soon we were out of the range of the stones.

Zoltán cried. He wept loudly and through his tears he muttered, 'Unclean! Unclean!', as he looked at me and Robert in turn. He gazed at the leprosarium, the trees and the old wooden cross on the front of the building. We sat him down by the fountain. Mstislaw came with a jug of water, put it down on the ground and disappeared back into the black hole that was the main entrance. No one, apart from him, came out to check what was going on. I imagined that everyone had seen from above what had happened and was now sitting in the loneliness of their shady rooms, plucking those words out of their hearts, those words that stabbed like sabres. It was all just another confirmation that we did not belong, a testimony to the vast desert of disease, fear, ugliness and disfigurement that divided us – Hansen's children – from the rest of the world; whoever tried to cross that waste would be stopped. Yet Robert was becoming convinced that it was worth a try.

The workers' singing moved away. We took Zoltán up to his room and laid him on his bed. The protesters had now stopped at the giant portrait of Ceauşescu and were hurling red paint and lumps of earth at it. From a distance it looked as if the portrait on the rough wall was being riddled with bullets and blood was streaming from it. Cheers came after every hit, and soon the face was covered with a mess of red and black blemishes. With the lumps of clayey soil sticking to it, it was reminiscent of a leper's face in the advanced stages of the disease.

I must say that Robert, ever the pragmatic American, viewed the events with considerably less emotion and associations. His version of the episode with Zoltán and the protesters would turn out to be more rational; closer to reality, perhaps, but less interesting. I guess that is how the world works, and literature too: stories are always written and remembered by people like me, not by the Roberts, Zoltáns and Mstislaws of the world.

We were still sitting in Zoltán's room when we heard the first shot from the direction of the factory. That instant the chanting turned into incoherent shouting. A column of police vans galloped towards the factory amid a cloud of dust. The foot of the chimney and the factory yard was shrouded in a downy haze of tear gas, from which bewildered workers emerged like ants. The wounded face of the dictator leered amidst the swirling smoke. A burst of fire from the top of the storehouse brought down two workers in overalls, who had hurled stones at the riflemen. The vans came to a halt a few hundred metres from the factory and riot police sprang out armed to the teeth and equipped with gas masks. With steady steps they approached the remnants of the discontented proletariat, and a gunshot resounded for every stone that hit their iron shields.

The bravest of the protesters hurled themselves against the battle-ready police cordon with cries of hatred. An iron door would open briefly and the charging worker would disappear beneath the truncheons and boots before he could even let out a scream. Most of the workers fled across the large field of young wheat south of the factory, but we could see from the leprosarium windows they were heading straight towards uniforms deployed around the long granaries at the end of the property.

The smoke soon dissipated. Ceauşescu could now observe the situation unhindered. Seven or eight bodies lay scattered about the factory yard. Those who had not managed to flee were now kneeling with rifle barrels trained at their heads. The police officer stood on the bonnet of a jeep and announced through a megaphone that all those who had been captured were to be considered criminals who had attempted to threaten the integrity and constitutional order of the Socialist Republic of Romania. They had also impugned the image and achievements of the President. Several workers tried to get up and speak, but the butts of the semi-automatic rifles were faster.

Robert also saw two policemen take the cameraman from the national television station behind the building. They slapped the poor fellow in the face several times, took out the video cassette and smashed it against the wall. One of the policemen patted him on the shoulder, and the cameraman inserted another tape. Everything went quiet again. The workers were probably able to hear the humming of the camera, the slow unwinding of the celluloid which now captured their frightened faces. With his truncheon, the officer pointed out to the cameraman who he was now supposed to film. The objective obediently followed and the large glass eye was held up to the bent heads of the offenders. Robert later commented on the bitter irony of the word for a glass camera lens, 'objective', being the same as the adjective describing a real situation or events. He was amazed at such a crass disparity and mentioned several similar examples which I no longer remember.

Zoltán finally fell asleep. Thick clumps of blood dripped from the fingers of his hand which hung by the bed. In his drawer we found a Bible, two ampoules of thiosemicarbazone and a syringe, and Robert injected the medicine into Zoltán's swollen artery. As he leaned over the old body, he smelt the awful stench which bore witness that Hansen was delivering its final blows. The disease was now rampaging in the disintegrating tissues of the old body. Zoltán had managed to hide its progress with his linen robe, silently bearing the pain. Next to his syringes there lay a faded photograph; the tiny child in the bottom left-hand corner with neatly combed hair, a cheesy grin and the lights of Budapest in the background was identified as Ingemar Zoltán on 13 May 1911. We looked at the child's slender arms. A wooden toy hung from one hand, while the fingers of the other seemed contorted; perhaps the boy was preoccupied with his fingernails. Even given the state of this 'child' today, there were evident similarities: the broad forehead, big dark eyes, long legs and prominent cheekbones were the same as the leper Zoltán's. We put the photograph back and tiptoed out of the room, both thinking of the child that lay like a ghost near its dying, adult reincarnation.

A group led by Mstislaw waited outside the door. They asked us how Zoltán was. After convincing them that the old boy would be alright, we all went off to lunch. They slurped their broth without speaking. They were waiting for Robert and me to explain the tumultuous events of the morning. The cutlery rang quietly to honour the workers who were killed. Police sirens passed the leprosarium on the road. Our glasses trembled from the rumble of lorries full of arrested protesters, so we did not hear the steps in the courtyard, the breaking open of the door of the ruined Baptist chapel, its loud closing and the frightened conversation of two unfortunates who had escaped the truncheons.

We split up and went off to our rooms after a lunch seasoned with Robert's reflections on the global crisis of humanity, the evil that affected all and the deformation of communist ideas in the countries of Eastern Europe. Each went off absorbed in thought, admiring Robert's eloquence. Some of his long sentences actually made sense. Like his claim that the fate of civilisation was inseparably tied up with the five percent of people gifted with the desire and the drive to use their lives to resist the temptations put before them by the dark side of the 'totality of our existence', as Robert called it.

I lay and stared at the ceiling. Robert was down in the courtyard reading. All the events had mussed up my mind like the wind tangles a girl's long hair, and I could not go to sleep. A day that began with the yellow daffodils was becoming a spiral of anxiety that intruded into the peaceful everyday life of Europe's last leprosarium. Although a mild spring sun was shining and sweet smells of verdure filled the air, no one else went outside. The only sounds from the courtyard were Robert turning his pages and the rustling of blackbirds in the bushes by the fence. Occasionally, the sirens of a police car would come from afar like the howling of the wind and then soon turn into thousands of glassy whispers.

The dilapidated Baptist chapel stood on a foundation of old reused bricks, so the ravages of time had easy work to turn it into a slumped mass of building materials susceptible to spontaneous collapse. I looked at it on mornings after windy winter nights, expecting to see it turn to dust before my eyes. Yet it survived. It was as if the rusty, iron cross which came out of the altar and up through the boards of the roof were a spine keeping it upright. Margareta Yosipovich had taken care of the building before she withdrew into her hibernation without return. Zoltán remembered the splendid pale-red roses and the little lilac bush, the clear and impeccably clean panes of glass in the small round windows and the smell of incense which Margareta received in Red Cross parcels. She knew several chapters of the Bible from memory, and if you walked in the courtyard you could hear a gentle muttering of holy words that filled you with peace. With her last strength she chained the doors together and virtually crawled back to her room, from which she was never to emerge alive again.

That chain no longer hung in its place, and the peace of the Baptist chapel was disturbed by the panicky whispers of the two fugitives, whose pupils dilated in fear whenever the wail of the siren filled the air. They assumed the police were hunting for them and were determined not to give up easily. Sitting on the edge of the fountain, Robert was the first to notice the distinct creaking of the old floorboards, a sound that couldn't have been caused by the wind. It came from inside, from the heart of the decennial darkness that preserved the cherished souvenirs of Margareta's unshakeable faith in God. He pressed The Bible against his breast and at that moment wanted to kneel before the altar and feel that special cold that only churches possess.

But the doors began to open before he even touched them. My friend looked on in wonder, prepared to believe that they had actually been moved by a divine force. Two heads with mops of black hair stuck out, one above the other, their eyes red and puffy from the tear gas. The Second Book of Kings: 'And the sons of the prophets said unto Elisha, Behold now, the place where we dwell with thee is too strait for us. Let us go, we pray thee, unto Jordan, and take thence every man a beam, and let us make us a place there, where we may dwell. And he answered, Go ye.' Shoulders with blue overalls also appeared.

I peered from among the daffodils on the windowsill and saw their hands fearfully signal for Robert to come up, and then not to come any closer. They gesticulated with their bodies, clenched their fists and contorted their faces, all so as to explain that they wanted to stay there in the dark. Robert nodded to show them he understood. He offered them the Bible to read, to alleviate their fear and the painful wait, but they did not want to take it. They needed only the dilapidated roof of the Baptist chapel; for they believed the police would not search for them in this accursed place.

Early in the evening a patrol car with flashing lights arrived at the gate. Robert and I were sitting on our beds, once again discussing the events of the morning. He accused the police of unseen brutality, but also thought that the workers had been rather primitive in expressing their discontent. I maintained that mass protest was the only way to gain attention and stand up against suffering, but he replied that it only reflected a questionable type of collective bravery that was incapable of articulating any rational goal, let alone attain it. A police officer called out from the gate, not daring to pass beyond the fence. He demanded that someone come out and only stopped his hullabaloo when the two of us appeared at the entrance. He made no effort to hide his large pistol but kept it stuck in his trousers. Its handle poked into his protruding belly.

Did we know what had happened? A group of criminals had tried to destroy the factory. Almost all of them had been caught, but several were still at large. Had we seen them here near the building? Or in the building? This hole seemed like an ideal hiding place. It was much more dangerous now that the fugitives were on the loose. We would be at grave risk. And the disease, it was contagious...

He spoke without letting his eyes meet ours as if we were evil gorgons who would turn him to stone, or even worse:

into a leper. Huh! His colleague was sitting in the car polishing his revolver on his sleeve. I thought of the wretches in the chapel behind us who were trembling like hunted rabbits. They were probably cowering beneath the damp floorboards, imagining what would happen if they were arrested. Their whole life long they had heard tales about the infamous catacombs of the Securitate headquarters in the capital; about torture methods that left the victims shitting blood for the rest of their days. That was not the destiny they wished for.

Robert made a jerky move towards the fence and the police officer jumped back in fear, reaching for his pistol. When I casually spat a large lump of phlegm on the ground, the fellow took another step back. His fear encouraged us. We realised he was not going to come anywhere near us. It was the disease that held him back. He looked at the lights up in the windows for a few seconds and then returned to the car, growling 'Damn lepers', or something to that effect. Robert flung back some juicy abuse in American slang full of 'fucking' and incomprehensible expletives. The wheels screeched, splattering us with mud, and the blue flashing light disappeared down the road, illuminating the fresh foliage of the bushes.

Robert and I exchanged glances and rejoiced in our victory. It had not been spiteful resistance to the arrogant force of the law as much as the desire to be part of something that existed beyond the fence. I don't think our quarrelsome impulses and gestures of rebellion against a small representative of Ceauşescu's regime were essentially any different to Zoltán's running out to meet the protesters. We all wanted human contact, even if it be conflict, so as to break down that fence that was much taller than the one around the leprosarium. If only for a moment. But everything foundered on the iron curtain that Hansen, like a devoted tradesman, had been erecting around our vile name for thousands of years. I could cope with a fat truncheon on my nose better than the habitual, 'Damn lepers'. I would have preferred the fat cop to pull his pistol and give me one big humane slug of lead.

In the eyes of our leper community we were heroes. When Cion ladled out the soup for dinner he adorned our plates with the largest pieces of boiled potato, and as a prize we were given two tins of pineapple from the kitchen storeroom. But no one mentioned the Baptist chapel and the fugitives. And why should they? Their silence was a way of telling us that it was our business and that they did not want the men inside the leprosarium. Using my authority, I decided I would allow the workers to sleep the night in the building, though I feared it might disquiet those sensitive leprous souls. The presence of healthy people offended them and put them in a bad mood, and I did not want to offend anyone, especially the freaks I had come to love over time, or even those I had learned to hate and similarly forgot to offend.

We waited for the night to take hold and then approached the rickety door. When we entered, Robert lit a candle which made our coarse and mutilated faces seem even more terrible. The two unfortunates lay huddled up against each another. They slept with their mouths open, making an odd chirping sound. The chapel stank of their sweat and the bad smell of the long gumboots left next to the altar. Above their sleeping heads rose the immaculate figure of the Mother of God; the dampness was making her paint peel. What gentle eyes, I thought, and held up the candle. All along the smiling mouth I noticed patches of greenish mould, giving her face a grimace like an expression of revulsion. I followed her shoulders and arms down to where they should meet as she held her child. But in place of the blessed body of Christ I now saw two Romanian heads. They opened their eyes and glimpsed the last thing they wanted to see: ghostly visages of Hansen's children lit up by the ruddy glow of the flickering candle. They cried out, making Robert stumble in his fright. The candle fell from my hands to become part of the heavy darkness and, for a moment, there was only silence.

Tripping over each other, the workers knocked over the altar in their rush to get out. They bumped into me and Robert too. Every bit of body contact increased their fear, and when they finally reached the door and kicked it open, they sat down on the ground and started taking off their clothes. Their eyes were full of fear as they looked around them, and their naked behinds now rolled in the sand. With every step we took they moved back two, crab-like; then they jumped up and started to run. We followed them as far as the fence which they cleared in one bound and then continued leaping over small bushes and puddles. We watched the gleam of moonlight on their sweaty backs for quite some time until it was lost amongst the thin tree trunks of the young forest. I was filled with a kind of disappointment paired with envy. I had really thought that those fools would condescend to talk with us and make an effort to conceal the revulsion and fear our illness provoked in them. That they would laugh with relief when they saw through the rickety door of the chapel that it was just us coming, and not the police. As I watched them stumble and fall, get up again and run even faster, I wished it was me who was fleeing from bloodthirsty police dogs through the bogs and marshes of this dreary country, hiding among the birches and breathing the damp odour of peat.

Before I went off to bed and fell into horrible nightmares filled with images from my childhood, I went to see Zoltán again. He was sleeping facing the wall, his arms pressed firmly against his chest. The creased and dog-eared photograph peeked out from between his fingers. His drawer was open; it held the dark emptiness of a life that was fading together with its memories.

When I entered our room I thought at first that Robert was kneeling and praying. He did not turn around but only waved; holding a sharpened lead pencil in his hand. The old map of Europe was billowing across the floor. He traced roads and rivers, marked towns, skirted mountains and big cities as if he were drawing in the route of a huge army. I asked him what he was doing, and in reply he drew two stick figures two or three centimetres north-west of Bucharest. Everything seemed so close. If I put my heel on the broad Transylvanian plain and pointed my foot towards the west, the tips of my toes would be somewhere between Bonn and Frankfurt. But if I took another step or two forwards, my feet would again be standing firmly on the rickety floorboards. Was it worth taking a step? What would a journey to other places bring? Robert rolled up the map without speaking, and the rustle of its precisely marked paper drowned out all the questions I wanted to ask.

CHAPTER FIVE

It's impossible to gauge the damage caused to lepers by superficial translations of the Old and New Testaments from Hebrew. Today it seems absurd to explain that the word tsara'th did not denote the disease caused by Hansen's bacillus, and that the Bible does not even give an adequate description of the symptoms of our misfortune. The Second Book of Kings (5:27), where Elisha heals the leper, Naaman of Syria, and punishes Gehazi by giving him the disease, says, '*The leprosy therefore of Naaman shall cleave unto thee, and unto thy seed forever. And he [Gehazi] went out from his presence, a leper as white as snow.*'

What snow? What rubbish. Obviously this was a disease that caused a lack of pigment – leukoderma or vitiligo, whereas my fellow sufferers and I can bear witness that our skin sometimes shows the opposite tendency.

In centuries past we were blasted by all manner of Christian anathemas, which overlooked the fact that Christianity itself was the main culprit for us rotting away in agony. It was none other than the crusaders, returning from their campaigns at the beginning of the second millennium, who introduced the disease to Europe. The continent was seized by the first great epidemic, which led the Third Lateran Council of 1179 to classify us as 'dead among the living' and to drive us away to wretched leprosariums. If you loved the Bible, you threw stones at lepers and hung bells around their necks: amusement for millions. We wore large yellow crosses sewn onto our left breast, and in some regions it was obligatory to shout, 'Unclean! Unclean!', whenever we went amongst other people.

Lepers who dragged themselves from market to market trying to elicit alms had to invest a lot of effort in making a stranger's hand reach into his pocket. The more skilful ones, often well-educated people abandoned by their family and friends, used their storytelling skills and sometimes managed to gather several dozen listeners. Considering that they never stayed in one city for more than a few days, their repertoire consisted of four or five stories, usually descriptions of famous battles or miracles which they had allegedly witnessed. At the beginning of the Middle Ages, the nobility recognised the recitation of these tales as a significant means of propaganda, and in some cases city dignitaries, and even members of the court, paid lepers to go from town to town and city to city spreading a particular story and enhancing it with embellishments and superlatives. Sometimes I feel I am doing the same thing, unravelling the tangled web which Europe's last leprosarium had spun over the many years of its existence. I do not know for sure what is hidden behind these sad palimpsests written by leprosy, nor what I will get when the essence of the matter comes to light. Perhaps just the compassion of the reader, or maybe the same expressions of disgust that have pursued us for centuries. Not that it matters: the past is crafted by a mighty erosion of time. New workers came to the fertiliser factory, Ceaușescu's face was freshened up with bright colours, and crows made a nest on the roof of the chapel. From the window I watched the dictator's vernal facelift which beautifully complemented the green landscape.

Red Cross packages arrived with considerable amounts of new medicines: clofazimine, which we used intravenously, and ethionamide in tablet form. At least one year of regular therapy was required for them to have any noteworthy effect. If we divided up the delivery into equal parts, it would last until late summer. Margareta renounced her share and Zoltán did too. He spoke less frequently and increasingly walked around near the fence, staring into the distance as if he knew exactly what he was looking at. Robert observed that his favourite place was a little marshmallow bush which he would stand by, fondling its broad leaves. He would devotedly pull out weeds around the bush, remove stones and look into the sky as if praying for rain. He too had become a vegetable. His meals consisted of several boiled potatoes and a small piece of rye bread which he ground with his rotten teeth. He stopped coming to the fireside gatherings and drinking the bitter elm-bark tea, and wiped his face with a dirty rag stiff from blood, pus and sweat. His nerve endings began to die off faster and you could see him kick a rusty piece of iron with his bare foot and laugh hysterically because he felt no pain, even though his foot was still bleeding. Robert and I caught him while he slept, and Cion cleaned and bandaged the wound, demonstrating the medical skills he had acquired in the Romanian army. We held Zoltán's hands until he went back to sleep, and then left the room without a sound.

On 13 June 1989, Zoltán did not come down for lunch. It was usual that he did not turn up before noon, so there was no fuss when the old man was an hour or two late. On the contrary, it was easier to eat without having someone at the same table picking scabs from his arms.

On the way back to my room I knocked loudly on Zoltán's door, but there was no reply. The bed was neatly made, his modest supply of clothes lay scattered on the floor, and the black and white photograph was missing from the drawer. Instinctively I took a look out the open window at the ground below because it all seemed more like a suicide than a planned escape.

We searched the courtyard, the chapel and the bushes on the other side of the fence, but found nothing. But Robert noticed that the marshmallow bush had been uprooted; presumably a sign of Zoltán's so-called 'madness'. The night was filled with pale moonlight and the barking of wild dogs. Worry and disbelief were heavy in the air. Sitting silently by the fire, I looked up at Zoltán's dark window, expecting any minute to glimpse the clumsy silhouette of the good-natured old man and for him to begin singing 'Back in the USSR' in his imitation English. No one spoke, and soon we broke up and went back to our rooms, preoccupied with thoughts about Zoltán.

I was woken by Robert shaking me. I got up grumpily, and he dragged me to the window. He pointed towards the gate, behind which the old man's body lay sprawled on the ground. The morning mist was drifting away to the west. It hung around the bushes and the verdant trees as if it were hiding from the sun that was about to come out any moment.

Zoltán lay barefoot, his feet bloodied, his face pressed into the ground. His skinny arms were outstretched as if in an embrace, the palms of his hands pressed hard into the damp soil. We turned him over onto his back. His linen robe and calico pants were torn and bloody in several places. There were prominent bite-wounds, and several chunks of flesh were missing from his right thigh. I had heard the dogs barking. They were Zoltán's dogs. Hungry midnight animals provoked by the rotten smell of his sick body. We had not paid them much attention when they hung around the fence at dusk. Someone would get up, throw a stone or firebrand, and the shining eyes would disappear into the bushes. Robert once tried to go up to them with a piece of bacon in his hand, but he was driven away by their harsh barking; they were hungry for something else. Nature has ordered things clearly: dogs are attracted by gangrenous vapours, the suppuration that eternally oozes from the excrescences and ganglions of Hansen's children, more than they are to a fresh piece of bacon or a veal chop. The unwritten law says that the dead have to be eaten first – the dying have to be sniffed out. And we possess all the signs that place us beneath a malignant shadow which can hardly be called life.

Without waiting for the sun, we carried Zoltán back to his room, wrapped him in a fresh sheet and laid him in one of the tin coffins taken from the attic. Lepers are buried together with all their belongings, so before fastening the lid of the coffin with four big screws we put in the few small objects we found strewn around his room: several pairs of neatly folded socks, clean handkerchiefs, a pipe with the Austro-Hungarian coat of arms, an empty tobacco box and the stuffed falcon that was attached to the head of his bed. It was as if we were burying a pauperised pharaoh, the last of his dynasty, a witness to the dissolution of a once opulent empire.

I had never thought that Zoltán would be the first we would bury here on the grounds of the leprosarium; there were more obvious aspirants to that dark throne.

The rest of the leper community waited in the dining room. When we appeared the whispering stopped. I saw there had been attempts to get specially dressed for the occasion; shirts buttoned up right to the collar and sleeves rolled down neatly. 'Our dear friend is no longer with us,'

I said, and my words were followed by loud sobbing and a high-pitched murmur. Robert and I entered the dining room and sat down. The empty seat dominated, and only when I tapped on the table did people's glances leave the wooden chair and the flowers that had been placed on it. It was not easy to agree to the details of the burial. We argued where the grave should be. Someone suggested I should give a speech accompanied by music from the loudspeaker. Others argued about the gravestone and epitaph.

Chairs creaked as everyone waved and gesticulated, trying to persuade one another about this or that, and Robert even grabbed a pencil and drew his vision of Zoltán's resting place on the table. I did not want to interrupt them because I knew that in talking about the old man's burial they were actually thinking about themselves; about the last act which would consign their miserable lives, to oblivion with dignity. Several minutes later they spoke openly about their wishes: flowers, large wooden crosses, religious rituals, and the place where they wanted to be buried. I withdrew, letting them enjoy their sweet thoughts about life after death and the secrets which would finally be revealed. They finished two hours later and went off to their rooms. They could not have had better graves.

When Robert knocked and came in, I was kneeling on the floor and steaming up the paper Danube along the Bulgarian border. We were to bury Zoltán at four o'clock. The others had already gone to dig the grave down by the chapel. The ground was soft and everything would be ready on time, Robert said. I held the map of Europe up to the window. It must have looked as if I wanted to compare the real picture with its graphic representation. The sun revealed little holes in France, illuminated blue blots of sea and red highways. How much longer were we going to rot in this hole with Europe hidden under the mattress, I asked. Robert was dumbfounded by my openness. Was he really as resolute as he had been that morning when he laid the passport on the shelf at my bed head? He told me this was not a good time; we could talk after the burial. He had plans, but everything was so discouragingly complicated. We'd talk later, he said once more as he left and closed the door with a bang.

I screwed up the map and flung it out the window. Then I rushed downstairs to find it, bring it back to the room and smooth it out again as best I could. After all, it was the only material link, a fragile bridge, between the desperate wish to leave this place and the roads I would have to travel. I spread it out on the bed and weighed down the corners with Robert's presents. He was downstairs directing the digging of the grave; others were looking for wildflowers along the fence. No one dared to go beyond the bounds of the leprosarium. The dogs had tasted human meat in the night, and we could assume that an insatiable craving was now smouldering in them to sink their teeth into it again.

Once a Bengal tiger has attacked and eaten a human being, it stops hunting other animals. The primordial gene of that same impulse had perhaps now been activated in these dogs. The isolated colonies of outcasts in northern India were decimated by the jaws of this wild animal, which caught up with the limping lepers with ease and dismembered them with a few powerful movements. To protect themselves, the lepers began to leave their dead out, unburied, which satisfied the tigers with abundant and regular repasts. This was a kind of pact with the devil, as it turned out, because if the tigers missed out for just one day they would attack under cover of night and wreak punishment for the shortage by biting through dozens of jugulars. The lepers thus began to supplement the animals' diet by killing the older lepers and later even the mute inhabitants of the lonely villages in the surrounding hills. It all thus came full circle: animals and people had the same mission.

When a special police unit came to set things right, the colony only had ten fear-stricken members left. They did not see the uniforms and automatic rifles as salvation but as a new way of satisfying the hunger of the evil gods of the jungle. They descended on the soldiers wielding staves and rusty knives, screaming at the top of their lungs. But a short and decisive burst of fire stopped them in their tracks, slugs of lead discharged at chest height. The colonel had a clear mission, he was to sort things out, and he had no particular instructions as to whether the victims should be animals or lepers. If he had shot any of the majestic Bengal tigers he would probably have incurred the wrath of a foreign-funded environmental organisation. This way the victims were the 'dead among the living' and everything was put right. Needless to say, the leprous bodies were gone when morning came; or so the legend says. And that legend, retold by Robert, made us sit in tense silence and listen for any rustling along the fence. There were no tigers in Romania, of course, but Zoltán's end echoed elements of that modern Indian tale and made it seem uncomfortably real. It drove us to dream with open eyes and listen to the ominous barking as a ring closed around the leprosarium.

Everything was ready. The grave had been dug, bunches of wildflowers picked, a sturdy wooden cross made, and Zoltán's remains carried down into the dining room. I put on a clean linen shirt and went downstairs. The others were already sitting around the table with the coffin on it. They were talking in whispers, as the burial rites prescribed, and sipping tea from enamel cups. Robert told me that we would be burying him at six o'clock and that I would be giving a speech. No problem, I told him, but why was there a cross? After all, the old man had been a Communist. Robert said he would replace the cross. He would make a nice stone slab with Zoltán's name engraved. Today they had to put something in the ground to mark the grave and it wasn't right that there should just be a pile of earth.

An hour later our procession began. Sobbing broke out when we lifted the coffin from the table. We carried Zoltán through the dining room and down the long corridor to the exit. The coffin was not heavy: lepers' bones suffer from a lack of calcium and connective tissue, so the weight of a man of average build is less than expected.

I saw the red sun sinking into the crowns of the trees and the wind brought acidic vapours from the factory's chimney as we headed for what was to be Zoltán's grave. The mound of soil was cast up on the right. And on it was a big black dog, just sitting there and licking its testicles. We stopped and put down the coffin. The bloodshot eyes watched us indifferently until I took a stone and flung it at the creature's snout. It got up and began to growl as if promising to return. It descended from the heap, raised its hind leg and released a jet of yellow at the foot of the wooden cross. Another stone forced him to trot off nonchalantly towards the fence; he cast us a glance and then disappeared into the bushes. As I spoke about Zoltán's virtues, his gentle nature and readiness always to return a smile, the muffled howling of the hungry pack came from the forest. That bestial requiem was the only music to accompany Zoltán's funeral.

We compressed the earth above the coffin as firmly as we could. The mound rose only ten centimetres as if we had buried just a small dog, not a grown man in a metal coffin. At that time, there was nothing to announce the coming rain.

We all went back to our rooms. Later we finished a brief, silent dinner and went to bed. Robert was first to withdraw under the blanket. When I came in I slammed the door on purpose in the hope that it would force him to keep his promise. He had said we would talk about everything later, but now he was pretending to be asleep.

I picked up a wet rag from the floor and tried to drive away a swarm of flies around the light bulb. Whenever I missed I would swear loudly, trying to attract Robert's attention. But he did not move, not until I hit him hard on the head; the rag descending onto his pockmarked forehead with a loud splat. He jumped and sat up in bed without a word. It looked as if he had been crying. He was about to speak but was interrupted by a mighty clap of thunder, followed by a flash of lightning that bathed our faces in a bluish light. A fly landed on his face searching for the nutritious secretions of his leprous skin. The little parasite stopped at the base of the nose, feasting on the trickle of bloody pus that ran down to his top lip. I offered him a clean white handkerchief from my pocket so he could wipe it away; Robert took it and gently dried his eyes. He really had been crying. Sitting on the bed, he looked much smaller than usual. His chin trembled as he tried to control his sobbing. I walked to the window and looked out at the roof of the chapel and the cross; I shifted my gaze whenever they were lit up by the lightning. The thin and unsettled surface of Robert's world, all the plans and thoughts that made the days at the leprosarium bearable, melted like fine March snow. His deep, self-confident voice had changed to an indistinct muttering that could not compete with the sound of the rain. In place of his sardonic smile, waves of despair and despondency now swept over his face, and when I called him he only shook his head.

The courtyard was covered in thick layers of mud. As I walked I lifted my feet high off the ground. Big drops of rain splashed on my bare head. I reached the southern wall and waited for another flash before continuing. The seventh stone from the left in the sixth row from the bottom. My passport was where it was supposed to be. The lightning flashes photographed the surroundings ever more often now, freezing the branches and fallen leaves. Zoltán's grave was in the midst of a round puddle, and when the lightning powerfully illuminated the ground again I thought I saw that black dog on top of the grave mound. It was digging crazily, with its voracious tongue dangling. I yelled out, not knowing whether I was driving away the animal or an apparition. I squelched down the corridor, leaving thick muddy footprints. I wanted to show Robert the passport and ask if he had forgotten the whole business of leaving which seemed to me more and more like a tiger lying in wait, a muscular beast which we had no hope of fighting. It now had one large paw on Robert, and unless he evaded its grasp now we would be buried here till kingdom come.

I took off my shoes. He was sitting on his bed, smiling, as he turned the map of Europe into a pile of little paper shreds. When he had torn up the last pieces of Scandinavia, he picked up some irregularly shaped pieces and tried to recognise where they were from. I opened the damp passport and held it in front of his nose. I told him I would consider him a hopeless coward unless he pulled himself together and reconsidered his behaviour. The black cloud floated away across the plain, leaving thick, fresh air behind it. Robert had stopped crying. He asked me to close the window. It was getting cold. I went off down to the dining room to get a cup of tea. The muddy footprints had dried and were now like the footsteps of a Man Friday. If I had followed them, I would not have been surprised if I had ended up in a completely different room or another world; they really looked so strange.

Robert's hands trembled, creating a miniature storm on the surface of the tea. Finally he managed to concentrate his gaze. He stared at the scattered shreds of Europe and sipped the tasteless liquid. I did not insist on conversation but he began to shake his head and tell me that I had already heard what he had to say many times. Mr Smooth was able to guarantee transportation. Robert took a sip of tea. We would be taken in a Red Cross lorry, the driver was easy to bribe. Robert picked a piece of elm bark from between his teeth. We would use minor roads so as to avoid police checkpoints and army patrols. That would take us all the way to the Danube. Robert put the cup down on the floor. All we had to do was decide where to go after that. Mr Smooth would put us on board a dilapidated Russian tanker with a two-man crew heading for Vienna, later to return to a harbour on the Bulgarian coast. Robert picked up the cup again and ran his fingertip round the enamel rim.

My heart was pounding. Beads of cold sweat dotted my forehead. It was not plans like this that scared me but

Robert's compelling resignation that had turned the Blue Danube into a cup of insipid, cloudy liquid under his nose and reduced Europe to a heap of shredded paper. I stood with my arms flung wide, and he threw himself onto his bed, covered himself with his blanket and cold-bloodedly wished me good night. If I had had a stick or a knife just then, I would probably have killed him without thinking twice. Just as he had cut the throat of my hopes for an escape from this place. I sprang onto the bed and straddled him. My hands went straight for his throat. I squeezed and paid no attention to his knees which drummed against my back and burst the swollen blisters there. I thought he would be stronger and would easily free himself from my grasp. He was frightened. He waved his arms, begging me to let go, but I did not stop. I watched the jugular veins on his neck and the swollen capillary network across his forehead with curiosity. They looked like rivers flowing together, like a map that had surfaced from beneath the skin. He began to whistle through his nose, and in spite of the pressure I heard that familiar melody, '*I am a poor wayfaring stranger / Travelling through this world of woe*'. I accepted this as a message of repentance and released my grip slightly. Robert tried to grab me by the nose. 'You fool,' he said. 'Where will you go? Got a wife with nice tits and a warm bed just waiting for you? Friends, maybe? Huh? Do you really think there's any other place for us? Huh?'

I looked daggers at Robert and wanted to put my hands back where they had been. He was still talking nonsense, but now without struggling. Drops of blood trickled from his nose. He tried to wipe them away but only smeared them over his face. I called him a stupid arsehole. Could he not see that the only thing in our lives still worth doing was to leave this place? He answered with a cynical laugh.

I replied by slapping him in the face, and he giggled even louder.

I didn't mean to really hit him, but I was overcome by a wave of sadness that rose from somewhere deep inside. I felt like running away that very moment, dashing naked across the field like those two stupid workers. I would jump over stones and wade through the wheat field, devouring the endless dark of the Romanian plain. The grass would sting my legs. A herd of horses would stampede when they heard my pounding feet. I wanted a full moon to appear on the horizon as well as clouds that travelled south. I would screech joyously like a hawk. No, scream like an Indian chief in his feather headdress. It would be like flying. Great fires were burning far away in the west. Who were the people that sat around them singing? I stopped, lit up by the red light. They called to me to join them. A tender warmth ran all through me. The women had big breasts and breast-fed handsome babies. A girl started to dance. The others clapped their hands rhythmically and watched her wonderful body. Everyone was attractive and healthy. But the merriment was interrupted by a commotion, at first faint, then ever louder. The children began to cry. The women whined in fear. No one paid any heed to me anymore.

Then a howling and wailing came from out of the darkness. The men kissed the children farewell and signalled to the women to turn the other way. The fires went out, and we heard the howling at the very edge of where the circle of light had been. A bloodthirsty growling grew louder and big black dogs jumped right into my dream. Robert shook the bed hard and forced me to open my eyes. There was still dried blood on his face, and I was about to open my mouth and ask him if he had been by one of the fires too. He held his head close and said that something was happening down in the courtyard. Leaning out the window, he pointed to Zoltán's grave; he thought he had seen a dog. That black one. He called for me to come and look and I tottered towards him, pursued by the tail-end of my dream. A full moon had come out after the storm, making the smallest of things visible. A heavy silence hung in the humid air outside. I told him I couldn't see anything. I stared into the darkness for several seconds more while Robert sat on his bed. His feet played around with the remains of the map on the floor. He smiled when he found the piece of Germany with Berlin on it. He apologised for his unacceptable behaviour and said that he had never felt that kind of doubt in his life before. I asked him to explain what these doubts were about, but he kept saying what a mess his life was and how absurd it was to try and do anything to rectify it. In the end he waved dismissively and said that he had decided we ought to leave after all. He thanked me for the sobering slap in the face and rubbed his reddened cheek. I said I was sorry, I hadn't meant to hit him. He told me that no one had hit him like that since his captivity in the cellars of Berlin.

I think that was when I hugged Robert for the first time.

We spoke until first light and then went to sleep peacefully, secure now in our seemingly clear decisions, precise plans and hopes for a better tomorrow. A little hole in Zoltán's grave the next day was the only thing to remind me of the bad dreams of the past night. The dog had been there and desperately tried to reach meat.

CHAPTER SIX

Summer was passing. Robert was around less and less, but I did not want to bother him with questions. I watched him jump the fence in the late afternoons. I assumed he was going to secret meetings with Mr Smooth to make arrangements for our departure. Every evening when we turned off the light I expected Robert to speak and explain what was going on, but he was tight-lipped, and I did not want to seem overly curious. I did my best to make good use of my time. A month's hard work and Zoltán's gravestone was ready to be raised. Another fifteen days and the mound was adorned with a mosaic of stones which I had brought from the rubbish-heap at the factory. Several of the patients, led by Mstislaw Kasiewicz, were willing to help. We built up a large stock of firewood. Cion Eminescu found several rusty fox-traps up in the attic and dug them in along the fence in the hope that this would stop dogs from coming into the courtyard. Robert did not participate in the work but was always prepared to admire the results. I could not help but be reminded of The Little Red Hen.

He found out about the plan irregularly and in small doses. By the end of August I knew we would be leaving in two or three months. The whole plan had to fall into place before our journey could begin. I realised this when he told me that most people rejected the job regardless of the money. As soon as they heard we were lepers they threw up their hands in horror.

'Why did Mr Smooth have to find that out?' I asked.

'He's an honest Romanian who doesn't want to expose his fellow countrymen to a hidden risk,' Robert maintained.

'That's why he's trying hard to find a driver who used to have tuberculosis.'

It was a known fact that people who had had TB were not affected by Hansen's bacillus.

'I don't understand why you try so hard – the guy probably just wants to get as much money as possible.'

'He does not,' Robert assured me. 'He's a good man and wants to help. He's spent his whole life sending lepers to this hole. He's probably got a guilty conscience. Perhaps he wants to atone for it, and I have no problem at all being the object of his atonement.'

I was not happy with the way things were developing. I was alarmed by Robert's behaviour but equally appalled by my own indifference and acquiescence to his secret dealings. I cast him stern looks which meant that I would be at his throat again if he messed things up. But usually I was worn out by the day's work and in the evenings I had no strength but to ask in an exhausted voice: 'Everything ok?'

Yet, despite this fatigue, I felt strength returning to my arms. When I clenched my fists, clear lines of muscle stood out right down my forearms. The lesions had partly gone from my back, so I often sat in the courtyard naked to the waist. All that, combined with carefully dosed injections of medicine and large quantities of elm tea helped me feel almost healthy again. I had no trouble chopping large blocks of wood in half, and often felt the gaze of envious eyes that would withdraw behind curtains with a rustle and hide in the dark. If I was annoyed by the clumsiness of my helpers and yelled angrily, they would hang their heads and try even harder to fulfil the tasks I had asked them to do. Someone always came running up with a jug of cold water, and at dinner there was never any argument about who deserved the largest helping of potatoes or the biggest piece of meat. My tacitly approved leadership position had never been more pronounced. And I cannot deny that I enjoyed establishing order, diligence and discipline, and introducing new rules.

The other patients would be cleaning the fountain or raking the courtyard to remove small stones, and if I appeared at the window they would really lay into their work to demonstrate their loyalty. Along with all its advantages, this set-up was bound to have just as many shortcomings, as I found out when a cough and a temperature sent me to bed with a high fever. Robert sat by my bed massaging me with alcohol. When anyone tried to enter, he drove them away with ill-humoured grumbling and slammed the door. But some time around midnight he failed to close the door in time. Mstislaw wedged his big shoe in the opening, and the door was soon pushed open. 'We have to talk with the boss,' Mstislaw said.

'The boss?' Robert threw back at him.

'That's right, the boss. Now get out of the way and let us through,' the faggot said, coming up to my bed with three others.

Robert kept talking behind their backs: he had known that my ambitions would boomerang on me one day, he knew these fools in all their vileness; you could see the hatred and envy in their eyes; it was no coincidence that God had rewarded them with the disease. He yelled louder and louder, and then his voice shifted out into the corridor.

'Let me go, you shitheads!' I heard him scream. 'I'll kill you, one and all. You too Cion! I'll shove a chair up your arse!'

Then his voice was abruptly cut off. The corridor echoed to the sound of the heavy bolt of Room 42 down in the cellar.

The steps returned towards my room and stopped outside the door. Only then did I notice the group looking down at me. An anxious voice asked me how I felt and if I was better now. They were already missing me, they said. Today they had been unable to organise work properly. They had quarrelled unnecessarily about petty details, they said, their heads bowed as if fearing my censure. At that moment I forgot about Robert; what was going on in the room was pretty strange. One of them lowered his hand tenderly onto my forehead and then nodded to the others. That meant the situation was serious. They glanced at each other to try and agree who would do the talking, they nudged each other and whispered. One silhouette stepped forward.

'You know... We thought that... err... How should I say...' he stammered, before he was pulled back. Now a more resolute voice spoke.

'In view of your health, we've decided that someone else should take over your role.'

My role, he said, and I wondered what that meant. At that instant I was overcome by the urge to vomit. I coughed and pressed my hand against my stomach. I raised my head with difficulty, and a malodorous mass spewed from my mouth straight onto their shoes. They scattered into the corners of the room and held their noses. No one came to offer me a glass of water or a rag. They stood with their backs pressed firmly against the wall as if they were holding up the whole world. I vomited and vomited until my stomach felt like it was trying to expel itself, causing unbearable pain. The acid ate at the skin on my face. I fought the urge to scratch myself, itching and stinging all over. My fever subsided a little, but everything around me was a mess. I had goose flesh and a chill coursed through my veins. My reserves of strength that had accumulated over the summer months of sweating and physical exertion had now vanished into thin air. I looked down at my arms and legs with curiosity as they lay flaccid beside my body. I tried to move them, but they only shifted slightly and my muscles hurt. No one stood against the walls any more. They had backed out while I was retching on the floor and had left the door ajar. Cion's hairy arm later reached in and turned off the light. The leprosarium descended into darkness. But my thoughts arose like vampires heading for their nocturnal orgies.

My eyes adjusted to the lack of light. I could make out certain objects and focussed on them as if I were rediscovering the world. There were no sounds to break the muffled silence. With a little imagination I could be a captain deposed by a mutiny on a ship of ghosts. A worn-out sea-wolf condemned to spend the rest of his days on a deserted Pacific island surviving on mango and wild turkey. But every glance at Robert's bed with its white sheets crumpled up in the middle brought me to the verge of despair. The remnants of the map, still strewn under the bed, now fluttered around in the draught like fragments of a fey prophecy. Scattered European cities, parted seas and interrupted rivers rustled, and that murmur seemed to contain the caustic laughter of all the roads and paths, all the wondrous wilds of the East and the suave parks of the West, as they chorused: nevermore, nevermore, nevermore. We would get two lovely graves, one on either side of Zoltán's. With time, mallow would sprout and grow from the mounds, nourished by our decaying flesh. Only the occasional humble bumblebee would descend to pay tribute to our mouldy bones, hallowed not by teardrops but by trickles of dog urine.

I opened my eyes. Several fat flies were buzzing around my head. Reality was no improvement on my dream. Now that the dark was receding, I would have felt better there, six feet under, than where I was. Birds announced daybreak. A distant rooster shrieked at the rising sun. My bones sighed in pain, and belated remnants of the previous evening still stuck to my head. I did not know if Robert had really been calling me, or if I had just dreamed it. The door was closed. Locked too, I imagined.

I looked around, desperately seeking a glass of water near the head of the bed or on the floor, but all I could see were large drops of dew on the window-pane. They shone like diamonds with a strange blue light that gradually faded as the sun rose. I waited for the first sounds in the leprosarium. There should have been steps echoing down the hall, going to the dining room or the bathrooms. I was surprised to hear a knock at the door, the creak of the handle and the sound of slippers scuffing over the floor.

It was Cion, carrying a large jug of water. He said he had forgotten to bring a glass. Did I have a glass? No, I didn't. As soon as he came up to me I exerted all my remaining strength to grab his long linen robe and pull him closer. 'Careful,' he warned, 'It'll spill'.

I raised my head to the jug. My teeth knocked against the rim. Gulps of cold water ran down my throat. I felt them spread in my stomach, my heart beat faster, sweat covered my forehead. My free hand gathered strength. Gulping down the last of the water, I punched the bastard right in his grinning jaw. He staggered and fell down beside the bed. I thought that would have knocked him out for a while, but the blow was not so hard. He jumped onto the bed with all his force and grabbed me by the throat. I managed to hit him several more times before Mstislaw stormed in and pulled Cion aside. At that moment I realised what the new hierarchy was. Mstislaw Kasiewicz was the new sheriff with his own rules and demands. Yet it would be an exaggeration to say that the leprosarium had a clear structure of control where everyone obediently obeyed the little dictator and complied with his every whim. In fact, it all looked like a bad film. The problem was that they actually seemed to enjoy their roles and abandon themselves to them with a repulsive obedience: typical subservient arseholes. Unfortunately I had been the high priest, the trailblazer who by coincidence had set up this type of order in the first place, not suspecting that it brought some other genre conventions with it, like elemental changes of power and the excommunication of the ousted leader and his associates.

Mstislaw nodded sternly towards the door. Cion wanted to protest but Mstislaw slowly raised his finger to his lips. Cion left the room with his head hung low. Mstislaw closed the door and sat down at the foot of the bed. He folded his stiff legs with an effort.

'Are you feeling better?' he asked, looking at my feet. My fingers writhed; I wanted to get away from those eyes. He was ogling my body with satisfaction, lingering on my muscular chest and bulging calves.

'You look healthy,' he said. I pulled the sheet up to my chin. 'You needn't be ashamed, we're all glad,' he continued. 'It looks as if your illness, I mean the real one, is going. But you and I know that's virtually impossible. The beast in us is merciless. It goes to sleep for a while like a snake, but then it will lash out of its hole again, won't it?' He drew back the sleeves from his forearms to reveal deep scars and half-healed lesions that had eaten away at the skin and deep down to the bone. 'See? That's the sorcery of it. The wounds always look like they're going to disappear the next day. Eternal hope: it kills us as much as Hansen does.'

Yes, that hope, I thought. He stared up at the ceiling as if he were looking for cobwebs. Or for God. He straightened his robe. His right hand went deep into its folds, he lowered his gaze, and his crooked, hairy fingers came out with my passport. He exulted like an amateur magician who had just pulled off a successful trick. 'We were looking for cigarettes in the drawer,' he said, returning the passport to its hiding place close to his body. He got up painfully and limped to the window. I did not make the same mistake a second time; I knew Mstislaw could easily overpower me in my current state, so all I did was give a vacuous look of disappointment like I imagine you see on the faces of people who are dying. 'It will be in my safe-keeping until you get better,' he said. Then he asked me if I wanted any more water, shambled to the door and was gone. His unsteady steps echoed down the hall and he whistled Albinoni's tedious Adagio. He could not reach the high notes, so he returned to the beginning over and over again. His whistling went out into the courtyard, and the melody wandered idly beneath the window. Albinoni was accompanied by the sound of urine splashing down the wall. The refrain quivered as he shook off the last drops. He did not stop whistling until the bell rang for breakfast. Then the creak of doorknobs was heard and the first conversations about last night's travails began: about pains in the back and bleeding from the anus.

I had enough strength to get up. The fever was gone and I no longer felt the debilitating pain in my bones. Yet I stayed in bed and asked myself if there was any point getting up. Last night's turn of events had robbed many things of their meaning, and I had yet to adjust. The thing for which I had been prepared to throttle my friend Robert had now happened. Now he sat humiliated on the damp floor of Room 42. He was re-experiencing the harsh captivity which this time could drive him mad. It had been a mistake to ignore old Zoltán's words and wave dismissively when he said they were all closet criminals, corrupted beings with the souls of ravens.

Now one could easily imagine them circling and driving out all the good and human kindness that remained in these walls, in the graves and the earth. But before I let my mind wander off in that direction, I heard someone calling for Robert down beneath the window, at first quietly, then louder and louder.

I didn't recognise the voice, as it was hushed and distorted. When the man had called out my friend's name for the fourth time, he paused and lit a cigarette. I heard the metallic sound of the cigarette lighter and his first deep drag on the cigarette; 'Robert?!' he called again; then rapid steps receded. I knocked over the jug as I jumped up. My feet met a round puddle of water and several shards of the ceramic handle which stuck into the sole of my foot. I strode to the window in pain, leaving a trail of blood. Mstislaw now stood down below, and beside him Cion, with the others crowded at the entrance. Mr Smooth stopped at the fence, crushed the cigarette with his heel, and looked at us for several seconds. No one dared to speak or go towards him. Mr Smooth wore a wide-brimmed hat which shadowed his face, but I recognised him by the way he held his cigarette, wedged deep between his middle and ring finger. I waved to him, but he jumped the fence and disappeared into the bushes without looking back. Mstislaw shrugged his shoulders as if he regretted not having given the uninvited guest a more courteous reception. 'If your friend comes back again, you might suggest he stay the night. There's plenty of space in Room 42. A whole continent!' he said, heading back inside with Cion's arm over his shoulder. The silence was soon replaced by the clank of cutlery. I hoped Robert would barge in through the door any minute, swear a few times and go off to have breakfast. That would be the end of the nightmare, the bursting of the soap bubble that the wind carries surprisingly far; to the unknown and dark realms of human behaviour. I felt betrayed because these were no longer the same people, those tormented characters concealed in crippled bodies. Now they had become something else again. But what? Perhaps Margareta Yosipovich knew the answer.

When Cion went into her room that morning with a hot cup of tea, he was struck by a horrible stench that almost knocked him off his feet. He drank a mouthful of the tea and summoned up the courage to go up to the bed. It was then that he noticed Margareta had blue eyes and very long eyelashes. He noticed because her eyes were still wide open, as if in leaving this world she had caught sight of what we all hope for. I had last visited her room three or four days previously. She had been sleeping when I entered, and when she awoke she acknowledged my presence with several barely perceptible twitches in the region of the lips, reminiscent of attempts to smile. I sat down for a few minutes, just long enough for the old lady to go back to sleep, and then turned to tiptoe out again. What happened next, there in the semidarkness, all went so quickly; I think I glimpsed the theme of my future nightmares, or perhaps it was just a trick of the glaucoma in my left eye: as I wheeled around and opened the door, the draught caused the heavy window next to Margareta's bed to fall shut; there was a mighty bang and the window-pane shuddered. It sounded like something broke, but when I looked back it was not the closed window that drew my attention and etched itself into my memory. I did not even tell Robert about this, but Margareta's head was raised up high off the pillow. Her thin neck, leathery like a turtle's, held up her small jaws and the tangle of grey hair, while her large blue eyes glistened maliciously above a smile which revealed her rotten teeth. In the blinking of an eye everything returned to its former appearance, and an instant later I fled the room.

Margareta Yosipovich's death was a relief to me. However much I tried to rationalise, my primitive alter ego told me that an old demon dwelt in that twilight room, not a tormented old lady who longed for the last guest. Yet another, much deeper and more significant doubt began to grow in me that night. I was increasingly convinced that there were things in the leprosarium that I knew nothing about: a hidden side of things, an inversion of the existing order concealed in the rat-sewers of functional reality.

With these thoughts in my head I groped along the wall down the main corridor. Margareta was already in her coffin, which was on the dining table. I peered in from the doorway. I was glad the lid was on and the body concealed; I was afraid my imagination might prepare me another episode of hallucinations. I went up to the table and intentionally sat on Robert's chair. 'Is he still in the cellar?' I asked. Everyone except Mstislaw was holding a handkerchief over their nose because the coffin was emitting the old lady's last statement.

I ignored the unbearable stench and repeated my question. 'Where else could he be?' Mstislaw replied, 'Off on a business trip, perhaps?', and several handkerchiefs fluttered to creaky laughs. I got up to fill a jug of water in the kitchen and then went to see Robert. The bolt on the door could be opened from the outside. If no one prevented me from going down, that meant Robert's captivity had only been an innocent game of a conceited little dictator and his subjects. They all looked at me as I went past with the water.

'The burial is at noon. We still need to dig the grave. It would be much appreciated, my dear...' Mstislaw said.

I nodded and calmly kept walking. They watched me in silence as I left the kitchen. I stopped for several seconds in the hall and waited, but no one got up. I assumed this meant Robert's imminent freedom, his release from the prison within this prison. I walked as quickly as I could. Putting the jug down on the steps, I went up to the door of the cell. There I saw two things: Robert's head pressed hard against the bars just above the number 42, and a large padlock hanging from the bolt. I do not know what horrified me most – the purple bruises on Robert's face or the brassy shine of that fist-shaped lock.

When Robert saw me he began to sob and wiped away the tears with his palm. I did not know what to say. I grabbed the padlock and jerked it this way and that, which only produced metallic screeching. Robert pounded furiously at the door and pressed his forehead even harder against the bars. I went back for the water, moistened my handkerchief with it and reached in as far as I could to dab his face. I told him to open his mouth, then I poured some water from the jug, trying to spill as little as possible. Finally I asked who had beaten him. He said he did not know who else had been involved, but he was sure about Cion and Mstislaw. Mstislaw had hit him in the head. They had sneaked in while he was asleep. He had been woken by a hard blow to the stomach. Cion brought up a chair so that Mstislaw could sit, and then they questioned him about our plans for leaving. He had not told them anything.

'But today they'll be back. That'll be my last chance,' Robert said.

'Don't worry, everything will be alright,' I said.

'Has anything in my life ever been alright?' he laughed.

'Quieten down, they might hear us and lock us both up,' I warned.

'So what?' Robert replied. 'What does it matter? Can't you see it's all over now?'

'Mr Smooth came and will probably come again,' I told him. Robert kept laughing. He teetered around the cell and fell down in a corner.

I couldn't bear to hear him anymore. I needed peace. Even if it only be the peace of Margareta Yosipovich's burial.

CHAPTER SEVEN

The events that followed are engraved in my memory like a jumble of rough-cut scenes from a low-budget film. I went up into the dining room. The coffin was still on the table. The gurgle of water and the noise of pots and pans came from the kitchen. Most of the patients were outside in the sun. Spades cut the dry earth. Several lepers were digging and wiping sweat from their brows, and Mstislaw, his arms folded behind his back, supervised the work. He told those who were digging to get rid of a big stone that was in the way. They were to dig at it from all sides, remove as much earth as possible from underneath it, and then lever it out with the metal bars that had once blocked all the windows of the leprosarium and now lay rusting by the fountain. I strode out into the courtyard, stopping for a few seconds near the door so my eyes could adjust to the sun. Mstislaw beckoned amiably but without taking his eyes off the hole that grew ever deeper. He praised the diggers when they loosened the rock in the ground, heaved it out and threw it before his feet. The heap on the right-hand side of the pit gradually grew larger. After a layer of red clayey soil they hit something harder, a pebbly conglomerate. Mstislaw suggested that someone else get down into the pit and looked at me. The heat above the earth created a thick wrinkled haze that made it look as if his legs were not touching the ground but floating several centimetres above it. Sweat stung my eyes. My brain seethed, causing a strange popping in my ears. For a moment I wanted to be sitting beside Robert in the eternal shade of the leprosarium's cellar; I would press my forehead against the smooth stone floor and enjoy the chill that crept up through my knees.

Mstislaw picked up a spade and held it out to me with a gesture of mock begging. I could feel the heat of the pebbles through the soles of my feet, but it was equally hot wherever I trod. The moist floor of Margareta's grave was almost enticing.

He didn't wait for me to come up closer but threw the spade to me. It corkscrewed in the air. The handle was hot. I would never have thought that wood could get that hot. I stood there on the edge, inhaling the smell of the earth until Cion prodded me in the back: I had to hurry. 'We haven't got all day,' he said.

I felt as if I was about to dig my own grave. Balancing on the spade, I jumped down into the pit.

The ground at the bottom really was cool. I was in the grave to dig alone and the others came up to the edges, making it seem twice as deep. I was surprised how soft the ground was when I first thrust the spade into it. I threw out soil, trying not to look at the eyes which formed a frame around the sun. My head spun. I tried to concentrate on the digging and get the best footing. Mstislaw said something; the others listened attentively, but I did not hear his words. It was as if we were already divided into two worlds, the living and the dead. The large clumps of earth gave off vapour as I threw them into the sun. With a little fantasy, I imagined myself digging my way to hell. At some stage the membrane of the earth would become too thin to bear my weight. Flames would spout up through the cracks, I would fall down through them with a cry and the on-lookers would clap. Two words from Mstislaw returned me to this world: 'Enough!', and 'Out!'

Sodom and Gomorrah, I thought, reaching out my hand so someone would grab it and help me out. But everyone hung their heads. Mstislaw had things well under control. Everyone moved back half a metre and waited for me to clamber out like some antediluvian creature whose remains archaeologists discover deep in the rock. 'Nice grave,' Mstislaw said, 'It suits you.'
'Yes,' I replied, 'it's lovely.'

The grave came up to my chest. I set the spade in the ground behind me, pushed against the handle and swung my legs up to ground level. The siren from the factory sounded, calling the workers to lunch. I stood in front of Mstislaw, clenching the spade. The horrible noise stretched out the time like chewing gum. Something had to happen when the music stopped, I thought, and gripped the spade tighter. The wail gave way to silence, and slowly Mstislaw walked to the edge of the hole. He reached into the folds of his robe and withdrew my passport. Raising it high above his head like a trophy seized from the enemy, he threw it into the grave. At that instant a large magpie alighted on the roof of the chapel and chattered several harsh strophes. Mstislaw stooped, took a fistful of dry earth that trickled between his fingers and threw it into the pit, covering the red passport at the bottom.

Had it not been for Cion's sarcastic laughter at that point, I probably would have reacted differently. But that brought things to a head, and I will dream the next few scenes for the rest of my life: I bent over to see where my passport had ended up. Its corners were sticking out from under the little heap of earth, like a little grave at the bottom of the big grave. Cion's squeaky voice grated at my eardrums. The sun was at its zenith and hopped round the top of my head. I firmly gripped the wooden handle of the spade, opened my eyes wide so as to see Mstislaw better, and then abruptly raised the oval blade. It hung in the air for several seconds. Everyone looked at it. Everyone watched as it swung down towards Mstislaw's head and sliced into his face across the middle of the nose and down his cheek. Blood only began to flow when I withdrew it. There was a crunch of bone as I pulled it out. First Mstislaw's arms went limp, frozen in motion. He blinked several times and slumped to the ground in a sitting position, as if to take a rest. He was still breathing. Shiny bubbles of blood rolled from his nose. The red crescent on the flat metal revealed the fatal depth of the wound. Now blood filled his mouth and poured out down his chin, dripping onto the ground between his legs. His eyes followed the spots on the earth, which slowly merged into one dark stain. He let out a muffled cry, his left arm twitched, and that was Mstislaw Kasiewicz's last sign of life.

I only called this event by its proper name once I had retrieved my passport from the pit using the same spade, cleaned off the soil and put it deep in my pocket. Murder, I thought for the first time, looking numbly at the others, who all withdrew before my gaze as if pushed by some physical force. No one came near me: this bloody corrida was all mine. They took another step back when I picked up the spade again and began pushing the lifeless body. Several energetic shoves and it tumbled into Margareta's grave. I looked down and wiped the sweat from my forehead, took a deep breath and then shovelled the first spadeful of soil onto Mstislaw's stomach. After that it was easy. A little more and his legs disappeared. Then the torso. Now soil came right up to his chin. I realised I was putting off the moment when I would have to shovel the dry dust and clumps of earth onto his marred face, but it could not wait forever. Just a light swing and a heaped spadeful became a reddish cloud flying towards his head; it covered his open eyes.

No one ever found out why I suddenly stopped and threw down the spade. Not even those witnesses standing nearest knew, because of course the only witness was me. I soothed my conscience by concluding that there was no going back in all this and that Mstislaw's eyes just blinked due to some late, after-death spasm. There was no better way to explain away the movements of those believed dead. I tried to forget the rolling of his eyes, the shining reflection of the sun in them and the horror that filled them as the spadeful of soil sailed towards his face. I thought I would feel relief when he was all covered up. Now there were only contours in the soil instead of the body, like the rough-hewn beginnings of a sculpture of a reclining figure: my work of art. Yet it was unfinished, because the pebbly soil over the mouth began to move and then fall into the little hole. Mstislaw's mouth was opening, taking its last mouthful. I threw myself onto the heap and pressed down the hot earth with my body. No one was watching in the courtyard any more. Only Cion sat on the stone rim of the fountain and wiped away his tears with his sleeve. Several other patients peeped from the windows but hid in the darkness whenever I looked up. Soon the grave was level with the ground. The only sign of the digging was a damp stain that the strong sun soon dried to the same colour as the rest of the earth. This unsullied earth, I thought. I sat alongside, waiting for a wave of repentance to befall me; that dull pain in the stomach, possibly tears, dizziness, a headache... whatever. But there was nothing, only the thought that I had to free

Robert as soon as possible, and then dig another grave; this time for Margareta Yosipovich.

My eyes, scorched by the midday sun, could hardly adjust to the dark interior of the building. Silhouettes fled before me in the corridors and I heard rapid steps and the creaking of closing doors. Death had intruded and disturbed the peace of Europe's last leprosarium.

With the spade in one hand I groped my way along the damp wall leading to the cellar. I peered through the bars of Room 42 but my friend was not to be seen. I assumed he had fallen asleep down by the door. I stepped back a metre or two and gave a mighty blow to the padlock. The wooden door-handle burst asunder and a screech of metal resounded in the high-ceilinged space, and only then did I hear a squirming and a sleepy muttering from within. I removed the broken padlock and drew back the bolt. The opening door brought the stench of human excrement; Robert was sitting in the corner to the right of the door. He was shivering like a wet cat. I tried to take his hand and pull him to his feet, but that proved impossible. He refused all contact. I sat down beside him and let his head lean against my chest. He seemed to have lost a lot of weight. His cheekbones stood out several centimetres from his face, and on his neck I could have picked up the loose skin between my fingers. When I lifted him up and carried him out, the dim light of the ground floor revealed streaks of grey at his temples that had not been there the day before. It was easy to imagine Room 42 as a hole in time where my friend had spent the night writhing under the truncheons and harsh commands of the Nazis who had been here decades before. In fact, I would have preferred that, because Robert's account far surpassed the fairy-tale quaintness of my imagination.

I put him to bed and drew the blanket up to his chin. Cion was still sitting by the fountain counting his fingers. No one went near Mstislaw's grave, not even the black dog that had wanted to feast on Zoltán's remains. There was no sign of life in the leprosarium. Margareta's grave needed digging, but I was afraid to leave Robert alone. I could not help but feel we were still in a little boat caught in the tentacles of a huge sea-monster. He could easily be suffocated with a pillow in the state he was in, I thought, sitting down on his bed. To judge by the abrupt shudders of his head and the way his eyes were rolling, he was having a bad dream. He moved his parched lips, and whenever I tried to moisten them with a handkerchief he turned his head away and withdrew under the blanket.

He awoke abruptly, at the very moment when yellow fangs were lunging at his throat, going for the jugular. He was tied to the bed and could not flee. From whom? From what? He could not remember. 'The fangs are all that are left of the dream,' he sighed. He drank a little water and a mouthful of elm tea at my insistence, and then began to tell me about the events of the night before. I was not sure whether he was discovering another dream or telling me what had really happened. He was not sure himself. The only thing that was certain was the fright he had received, and the grey hair, and the several kilos of bodyweight lost as a result of his ordeal.

'I stared through the bars and felt the swelling on my face. Those fools sure beat the heck out of me,' Robert said with a sniffle. He rubbed his temples as if he could feel the white streaks with his fingertips. Sitting on the floor of Room 42 he had concluded that his life was one big misfortune. That had led him to reflect of his childhood, but only briefly. He would have blown his brains out if only he had had a pistol. The bullet would bore through his skull and make a dent in the wall whose surface he was fingering. His fingers felt carved letters in the stone. He could not read them, it was too dark. He fondled those words, perhaps a whole sentence of them, and wondered what had happened to the person who wrote them. Through the bars of the door a draught picked up. An open window or a door ajar could easily stir the air in the leprosarium. He pressed his face against the bars and let it be caressed by the air flowing in from the dark. Oxygen is good for leprous skin.

He closed his eyes and tried to clear his mind. But conscious efforts like that usually have the opposite effect, and soon his head was crowded with people, lips, the long-forgotten landscapes of his native Gainesville, Berlin streets, the taste of coffee and a few remembered words of German. He did not know what made him abruptly open his eyes; like a woman who has just dreamed that strangers have abducted her children. He heard a noise close at hand which, he now knew, meant the presence of some other being and not the movement of air. That person stood at the bars on the other side. He was sure he had never seen him before, but the person reacted with an expression of familiarity. Robert was frightened like a child that has just dreamed it is being kidnapped. He recoiled, slipped and lost contact with the floor. The back of his head smashed against the wall. His was afraid to open his eyes again. Every brain cell pulsated with pain. Millions of minuscule pulsars turned his cranial cavity into a galaxy of unbearable suffering. He closed his eyes and opened them again. The face was still at the bars: its grimace widened slowly to a spiteful smile. Harsh tittering and a salvo of unknown words filled the room. Robert didn't know how long that lasted, nor how it ended. He remembered putting his hands over his ears but was not able to stop the ghastly noise. He ran about the room, from wall to wall, until he fell again and lost consciousness. The next thing he heard was a blow on the door, the scrape of metal and my voice calling his name.

When he finished his story he leaned back against the wall and took Zoltán's Bible down off the shelf. He didn't read but simply turned the pages.

'Where are they?' he asked.

'Who?' I replied.

'*Thirty milch camels with their colts, forty kine, and ten bulls, twenty she-asses, and ten foals*,' Robert said, running his finger along the lines in the Book of Genesis. 'You know who - the faggots. I'm going to get them.' He wanted revenge. He would not calm down until he had beaten them bloody, both of them. 'They wanted to flee instead of us, they asked me about my contacts outside. But I'll send them where they deserve. They'll both rot in the cellar,' he menaced.

I hesitated to tell him about Mstislaw. I would have loved to tell him that the rat was dead and gone thanks to me. I would have told him that straight off, if only I didn't have to tell him about the brutality of it, for which, there was no real justification. Had my life been at risk? Hardly. That was what made me feel uneasy. In the end Mstislaw was butchered like an animal rather than slain in righteous rage.

The heat of the late-summer day was soporific. Robert's hands rhythmically leafed through the thin pages. Here we were again, back in the cosy cocoon of everyday life: the alluring simplicity of inconsequential days and the peace of this big grave were things I rather enjoyed. I struggled to keep my eyes open. But the little spider slowly spun its thread down the length of the wall. I fell into a dreamless sleep. When I awoke I was alone in the room. Robert was gone. The book stood opened and upright at the head of the bed.

A shrill voice came from the courtyard. At first it hardly sounded human. It made me think of an ugly, unnaturally large bird that was flapping around and burning. Who would harm such a bird?

I leaped to the window. Cion was crawling along on the ground with Robert prancing around him. Robert would kick him and bend down to say something, and Cion would whine and call for help. He wiped blood from his face, but Robert did not stop. He sought the most painful places: series of kicks in the ribs, then in head, then in the ribs again. I ran down the stairs and pushed my way through the crowd of onlookers at the door; stepping in front of Robert with my arms spread wide to hold off his attacks. He told me to move aside, he had a score to settle, he said. Cion grabbed my leg and pressed his head against my calf. I tried to step away, but ended up dragging Cion along with me. I told him to get off me, I yelled at him, but in his fear he would not let go. Robert was no longer trying to get at him but stood watching to see how my little drama would end. I pushed against Cion's head with my hand, trying to pry him off, but that made him cling on even tighter. Pain: for a moment I did not know where it was coming from and what actually hurt; I took one more step before I finally realised that the brute had bitten me and was clinging on with his teeth. If I did not remove him soon he would bite a chunk out of my leg. Punching him in the head was not the only solution, but it was the only one I could think of at the time. Whack, whack. But he just clenched his teeth tighter. I bent down and hit him with both hands. The parasite finally let go. I saw that he was giggling to himself in malicious glee. I turned to hit him again, but Robert was quicker: he came running up with a sharp-ended pole that made a kind of crackling sound. The bugger stopped laughing then. Blood flowed from a new wound. He turned his face towards the sun and squinted. I imagined that the star in his eyes had a splendid purple colour. I picked up Cion's limp hand and took his pulse. He whined as if he had been trampled underfoot, but he was still alive, the rat. His false foot had come off and lay several metres away. I fitted it back on his stump, and Robert laughed because I had put it on back to front by mistake.

I took Robert by the arm and we went back to the room. We met no one on the way except for the putrid smell of Margareta's corpse. 'They're frightened, the shits. And so they should be,' Robert snarled. 'Now you know who's boss around here,' he yelled.

'Who is the boss?' I asked him.

'We're the boss,' he said, patting me on the back. He felt much better. He was in a good mood again, and as we walked down the corridor he whistled his favourite tune.

Yet when I looked out the window and saw Cion dragging himself towards the door, I was overcome with pity. I was glad the old bugger was still alive.

'Robert, why did you have to beat hit him up like that?'

'I didn't mean to,' he said, 'I only had it out for Mstislaw, honest. Women, children and invalids? Never!' he swore. 'I met Cion in the corridor and asked him where Mstislaw was. The fool scratched his balls, or at least the place where they used to be. He wanted to know if I had had a pleasant night, and he asked it in that horrible whisper which is probably what has given me these streaks of grey hair. I suspect it was him who was shuffling around by the cell,' Robert said. 'I chased him around the room and caught up with him in the dining room. I dragged him out into the courtyard and... you know the rest.'

Robert straightened up his bed and said he would look for Mstislaw later. 'He's probably gone to hide in the chapel. But we've got more than enough time. He won't get away,' he menaced, smacking his fist against his palm.

'Mstislaw is gone,' I said, but Robert did not turn around to look; he thought I was just airing a threat. 'He's dead,' I restated. 'I killed him. With a spade. He's buried next to Zoltán.'

My friend smiled with incredulity. His doubt annoyed me. It also emphasised that he had not really wanted Kasiewicz to be killed: a dangerous step beyond the safe circle of permissible acts.

From then on I began to see myself as the motor force behind all these horrors; a little latch on the gates of evil. Robert had imposed the idea of leaving, and I had turned it into a rogue elephant which we needed to mount and leave this Atlantis of pain, without being heard. How can you re-tame an enraged monster?

Robert went to the window. He looked towards Zoltán's grave. 'There?' he asked. 'Next to the old man's?'

I nodded.

For a few moments my friend stared at me as if I was a brutal killer. Which in truth I was; at least in those few minutes when I broke Mstislaw's skull and buried him without even the usual futile rituals. I left Robert by himself and went back down to the cellar for the spade. The stench of the decomposing corpse now filled the corridors on our floor too: I had to bury her as soon as possible. I realised that I perceived the old woman as a kind of collaborator in Mstislaw's disturbances, and that was why I was not particularly gentle when I took the coffin down off the table and dragged it to the spot by the chapel. I dug an irregular pit one metre deep to swallow up the last memories of Margareta Yosipovich while Robert sat pensively in the shade of the chapel. From time to time he looked up. It seemed he had remembered something or wanted to say something, but soon he would be looking back at the ground again, tracing paths with his eyes that he alone could follow.

It was getting dark when I put down the tools. Big, red blisters filled with pus and blood had appeared on the palms of my hands. I slapped the dust from my clothes as if to free myself of this day. Nothing was the same any more, I thought, and invited Robert to come and join me in the dining room. I made a big pot of tea and sipping the hot drink returned the lost peace for a little while. We poured ourselves some more, and the gurgle of the tea was suddenly joined by the sad melody of the Romanian national anthem from the factory's loudspeakers: the workers of the second shift were lowering the flag they all hated.

I turned the lights on. Robert said it was nicer in the dark, so I turned them off again. He put down his cup. He still remembered that smell, he told me. Italian perfume in a surprisingly large bottle; reminiscent of expensive French cognac. Martha had liked to rub it in straight after her shower: a thick drop lay in the little valley of her palm. She spread it carefully and then ran her fingers sensuously all over her body. She once let Robert do it. Now I thought of Brahms's Hungarian Dance No. 6 and the loud laughter of a beautiful woman whose breasts trembled; fingers glided over her moist skin. I tried to imagine her lying on the dining-room table and me touching her magnificent body. I saw her breasts, the muscles and curves of her belly, but instead of full lips and rose-tinged cheeks my mind's eye saw only the horrible grin of Margareta Yosipovich, and that forced me to turn the light on again. Robert, surprised, wiped away tears and then kept on crying with his face in his hands. I realised there was no point trying to comfort him, and that made tears come to my eyes too. I left my friend and went off to our room. Several hours later, staring at the ceiling, he told me that he had been crying because of Martha. These were not banal memories of something beautiful that was gone. On the contrary: that night Robert had uncovered the bare bones of reality, hard and heavy, that had oppressed him for years. Now he wanted to share that burden.

Again the story about his brief but fateful confinement in Berlin, the event that had ruined his life, he recalled the malodorous cells, the shaven strong arms that dragged him down the long corridor and then up a flight of stairs. Until now he had never mentioned a door left ajar and a band of light that stabbed down obliquely to the floor. He had heard the conversation, he said. A satisfied bass male voice spoke politely with a woman. It seems the man told a joke involving a play on words. Robert did not understand the words, but he remembered that the young woman replied with a loud laugh; throaty rhythms well known to Robert and ending with a soft flicker of the voice. Robert hummed Brahms's Hungarian Dance No. 6, and I imagined six Martha Golbergs dancing and raising their legs high, can-can style. I imagined betrayal.

CHAPTER EIGHT

A certain Professor Horatius Portos Tercino, a prominent scientist and specialist in infectious diseases (he sounds more like a local football trainer in the Argentine Pampas to me and does not inspire much trust), claims that the oldest traces of leprosy have been found among the Australopithecus. Porous cavities in the cervical vertebrae of fossilised remains apparently prove the presence of Hansen's bacillus. With my right hand I rubbed my neck, with my left I turned the pages of the Medical Gazette (April 1985). The last passages presented interesting details from medical history. They said that over three thousand years ago the Chinese synthesised a kind of antibiotic from the leaves of a species of oak, since extinct, which they used to fight bacteria. Nonsense: I believe that reports like that are thought up by governments to maintain the human race's confidence in civilisation. Stories about wise, old civilisations are a mental crutch to help fill the septic tanks of primitive history, I thought as I pulled up my underpants.

A piece of blood-covered excrement lay in the toilet. Robert was still straining in the next cubicle, but the groaning I heard was not that associated with successful bowel movements that send a tingle of relief up your spine. Robert only emptied his bowels once a week, at best. His stomach was ruined, his digestion slow, and the muscles that supported the large intestine had atrophied, which was a common problem. I advised him to follow my example and eat large quantities of steamed nettles and dandelion leaves, but after he had eaten a few spoonfuls of the green mixture he would curse and spit out every little bit. That was one of the traits that I always admired in him. Unlike me, Robert never accepted even the most banal of compromises when it came to treating his disease. He consistently rejected the ampoules of a fairly effective digestive remedy which had to be injected into the buttocks and refused to treat the lesions on his face with his own urine. He bore the cross of leprosy with dignity, refusing to be a disease in human form, like so many others, and insisting on being a human infected with Hansen's bacillus.

He was pale and exhausted when he returned from the bathroom. He was still holding his belly and making a pained face: he had obviously been unsuccessful. This significantly influenced Robert's mood because it is not easy to carry around a sack of shit inside your body. We were imprisoned here, and he had to carry another prisoner inside him. He went out for a walk in the courtyard but avoided the graves by the chapel. Everyone avoided them, as if they housed the accursed victims of Vlad the Impaler, and not three worm-eaten corpses. I wondered to myself which was worse.

The August heat continued on throughout September. The bronze bust of King Alexander John I was an infallible thermometer. If you were able to hold your hand on the hot metal face for longer than thirty seconds, it meant that the sun was relenting. Whatever the outside temperature, the rays of the autumn sun were unable to heat up the old Romanian king to the same extent. But like I said, this September was an exception. Swarms of flies travelled restlessly in search of food. It was impossible to drive them out of the dining room and bathrooms. Every day clouds of the tiny kamikazes descended on your forehead in search of a mouthful of sweat. The northern wind, usual for this time of year, brought clouds of nitric compounds which caused a gentle burning sensation in the lungs. We had to wash the elm bark in cold water to get rid of the chemicals. There were no longer meals together in the dining room, nor fireside gatherings and the ritual drinking of tea. The residents came for their meagre daily rations and took them back to the solitude of their rooms. Only Cion went and ate by the grave of his dead friend and lover. He passed me and Robert as if he did not see us; until one afternoon he knocked on the door and said: 'I want to come with you.'

He said nothing to Robert's, 'Piss off, you pig'; only ducked to avoid the shoe, and then calmly repeated himself, closed the door and left.

There was no sign of Mr Smooth. I noticed that Robert went out to the fence every morning to look in the shrubbery and out at the foggy plain. There was a kind of tacit agreement between us: I would not ask about us leaving, and he would not mention Mstislaw's murder and the events that accompanied it. We were increasingly preoccupied with obtaining food because deliveries from the International Red Cross no longer came regularly. I assumed that the drivers gave the packets to the peasants in exchange for a chicken or a few kilograms of grain. The withered wheat and broken corn in the fields portended a hungry winter. All this led us to look with different eyes at the flocks of scraggy sheep that descended from the mountains. They were heading towards the cities to be milked some more, or else to be slaughtered. At first I didn't understand why Robert wasted several hours sharpening two large kitchen knives in the courtyard, but Cion skipped his meal by Mstislaw's grave that day, evidently frightened by my friend's possible intentions.

He woke me before first light, threw a knife onto the bed and waved to me from the door. Still groggy with sleep and confused, I thought my friend was going from room to room cutting the throats of our fellow lepers as they slept. I imagined purple stains spreading over the white sheets. A few managed to scream, but most were only able to open their eyes, woken by the warmth of blood and the sudden difficulty in breathing.

I was relieved when I saw Robert passing a number of the doors on the first floor, before continuing to the ground floor to sit down breathless and wait for me. Yet it still wasn't clear to me why he had to drag me out of bed so early in the morning. I shrugged and spread my arms, hoping for an explanation. Instead of using words, Robert held up the knife, pretended to draw it across his throat, bleated and pointed to the door. The flock was munching at the low vegetation and self-sown corn close to the fence: ewes with their lambs clustered around two big, horned rams, which were industriously searching for shoots of birch.

Robert pointed towards them and told me to pick some of the mint that grew in the shade of the chapel. I stuck my knife into the ground and started to gather some stems, when Robert came up to me and told me his plan. It sounded simple enough. You hid the knife in the bunch of fragrant leaves, lured the lamb, and as it nibbled at the aromatic herbs you slashed the knife back across its throat.

We jumped the fence. The sheep were evidently fairly tame; they kept munching the succulent green and hardly took notice of us. The sun had now risen and their wool looked blindingly white. Robert approached a lamb that had become separated from its mother. He cooed to it and waved his bunch of mint as if trying to hypnotise it. He checked to make sure that the knife was well hidden and then moved up close. When the unfortunate animal decided to take a first bite and greedily chomped on the leaves, extending its thick neck, Robert cut with a powerful movement at exactly the right spot. A spurt of blood splattered the fleece. The lamb made a different sound now; it began to run, and several seconds later Robert started off after it with his knife raised. The animal tried to hide under the grazing body of its mother, but she pushed it away with her nose as if she scented the presence of death and realised it simply had to be accepted. This Gandhian stance disappointed me. Instinctively I ran towards this sheep, grabbed it by the scruff of the neck and was just positioning the blade when a shot rang out. Robert grabbed the lamb, which was still dripping with blood, and started to run. The man was far away in the field. He fired another shot and several curses in Romanian. It was important to jump the fence; an imaginary border between two worlds, whose encounters always left ugly memories, or worse. That truism was confirmed this time, too. The smallish man with an unkempt beard went up to his herd, patted several of the ewes, and then grabbed the one that bleated the loudest by the scruff of its neck and dragged it away from the others. We understood it was the one that had lost its lamb. He cocked his rifle, put the barrel up to the sheep's head and pulled the trigger. The large-calibre bullet blew the animal's skull apart. Its legs twitched and it collapsed. We watched the man through a hole in the wall of the chapel. He came up to the fence and, without aiming, fired several shots at the building. The bullets struck the bare wall and left noticeable holes. He cursed the lepers and said he would kill every single one of us if we ever went near his sheep again. He walked away grumbling under his breath, and I had to restrain Robert from going up and sorting things out with him. 'Let him kill me straight away if he wants, the stupid arsehole,' he said, 'just like a sheep.'

We knew that the shepherd had killed the sheep because it had been touched by a leper. Had I been in his shoes, I would probably have done the same. We watched him as he chuffed away, leaving puffs of smoke behind him from his large pipe.

Robert's clothes were drenched with blood. He threw the lamb on the ground and stared towards Mstislaw's grave. A shallow hole had developed in the soil. The body, buried without a coffin, was rotting and making space underground. Robert looked at his hands and smelt his bloodied fingers. With his foot he pushed the lamb away, now coated in dust. He ran to the chapel, propped himself against the shaky wall with both hands and began to vomit. That was his real feeling about Mstislaw's death.

'I had to do it!' I shouted at him. 'Otherwise we'd both be rotting in the cellar.' Robert's stomach responded with a mighty spasm that ejected yet more green mucous.

I picked up the lamb by its front legs. Its head twisted to the side, further opening the deep wound from which a whitish artery and a bundle of cut tendons protruded. Human or animal – it's all the same, I thought, it's only the methods that are different. It's much harder to butcher a lamb, separated from its mother, than to kill an enemy at the front. It's worse to throw a live lobster into boiling water than to accidentally run over an old man crossing the road at the wrong place. Isn't it?

Robert went back to the room for a well-deserved rest. The dead lamb, the sun and a swarm of flies remained behind. The animal needed to be gutted and skinned, and I had to overcome my revulsion – after all, we were hungry. I tried to act as if I was resolute: I found an old piece of wire and bound the hind legs together. But what then? Suddenly I felt thirsty and went off to the dining room to drink some water. Lots of water.

I never asked Robert if he'd ever killed a man. I never really had occasion to ask. Today, I thought, he had carefully selected his victim and done some efficient knife-work. Those movements spoke of experience, it seemed to me. A bit of imagination and I could see him stealing up to a sentry. He sizes up the black silhouette and locates the arms, the weapons, the throat. He feels the warmth of the body, hears the breathing, the noise of a packet of cigarettes and the sound of an ignited lighter which illuminates the forehead. He closes his eyes because he does not want to see his enemy's face. The cigarette lighter is returned to its pocket; Robert's hand grips the handle of the knife. Two or three more silent steps, an outstretched arm, and the blade flashes...

I hung the lamb from the iron ring that protruded from the side wall of the leprosarium. I eyed the carcass, not knowing where to start. I could not decide whether to go for the stomach or the spine. The flies attacked, and I drove the blade into the cervical vertebrae. Drawing a line down the back, I took hold of the edges of the skin that flared outwards along the cut and pulled down. It sounded like thick paper being torn. Healthy, dark-red meat was underneath. I sliced down the legs, then stabbed into the stomach. The intestines fell out and stretched down to the ground. The liver and gall bladder hung entwined. The flies went wild, laying millions of larvae: a loud orgy of life. Breathless, I stood before the massacred carcass which had somehow stretched out and mutated. What used to be a lamb now looked like a dog. The stripped snout now had teeth, which made the creature look like it was laughing. I stuck the knife into the thigh and sat down to have a rest. But before I had even touched the ground I heard applause and a cheerful, 'Bravo! Bravo!' from the nearby bushes.

I was surprised to find I had an audience. The branches moved. I was expecting the bearded shepherd and a shot that would fell me or perhaps mutilate me further. Brushing pieces of dry leaves off his clothes, he came up to the fence: it was Mr Smooth. He had aged considerably. It was a long time since I first saw him close up. Now he jumped the fence and as he walked towards me he put on thin rubber gloves and offered me his hand. It reminded me what the handshake of a healthy body was like. Some traces of dried blood were now on the pale rubber. 'Good job,' Mr Smooth said, sizing up the lamb. 'I'm sure it'll taste good'.

Still I said nothing. I didn't know what I should feel towards him. The ball rolled and settled somewhere between hatred and a kind of 'pleased-to-see-you-again-because-you're-going-to-get-us-out-of-here'. He offered me a cigarette, then put the packet back in his jacket pocket without waiting for a reply. 'Patience, patience, just patience,' he said and lit up. The flame of the lighter was invisible in the bright sunlight. I asked if I should call Robert. 'No, old boy. Why? You're friends, aren't you?' I nodded. 'You can call me Martin. Martin will do.'

'Martin?' I asked abruptly a few moments later.

'Yes?' came his friendly reply.

'Nothing,' I said, 'Just testing.'

He put out his cigarette. His forehead was dry, but his hand was as cold as a corpse's. He gave the impression of being devoted to the tasks of his service. Yet I also imagined him a devoted hedonist, bachelor and lover of all manner of worldly secrets.

'Irina, my wife... You don't know her, unfortunately. Irina thinks lamb is the most delicious sort of meat.' He patted the red thigh and drove away the flies. 'But I don't eat meat. I'm a vegetarian,' he said, pointing to his breast as if he were proud of the fact. 'Otherwise I assume you'd insist on me staying for dinner?'

'Of course,' I replied, 'consider yourself invited.'

'Thank you, but I've no time. I'm just passing through. Assignments, duties, business trips – there are so many obligations,' he sighed. 'I used to pass by this way more often, but recently things have become complicated. I've been promoted, though it's doubtful I'll be in the position for much longer – times are changing and becoming dangerous,' he said, pulling the knife out of the lamb's thigh. 'I'm thinking of you. I'll fulfil my promise even if it costs me my life,' he avowed, and sank the knife in even deeper. 'When I come to see you the next time we'll leave together. I brought you here, and I'll get you out too,' he said, lighting another cigarette. 'There's now a driver, by the way: me.'

I was curious. 'When will you come, and how...,' but I was cut short.

'No, you must be patient for just a little longer,' he said. It seemed he was afraid of questions. He stubbed out his cigarette and jumped the fence. 'Remember: next time,' he called, before disappearing in the bushes.

'Next time,' I said, perplexed, nodding and raising my hand in farewell.

The white rubber gloves still hung on the fence, as if Martin's appearance had been part of a magician's trick. I thought I had better go in and tell Robert straight away, but there he was, coming towards me in a hurry. He fell to his knees and shifted his jaw; he had something to tell me. 'Cion...' he stuttered, 'Cion's killed himself'.

I was busy gutting the sheep and did not stop: now I had the heart. As I grasped it, thick syrupy blood began to drip out. Robert sat on the ground and watched the movements of the knife. This was the second time that Martin's visit had coincided with death. With a little fantasy, I could imagine him as one of its incarnations. I severed the lamb's head with a swift stroke. I was never partial to that kind of mystification. If I had to imagine an earthly embodiment of death, it would always be the old Galápagos tortoise with inflamed eyes which slowly but inexorably moved towards its goal. Its meaty insides spread an indescribable stench, from which both people and animals fled. I imagined just such a giant tortoise pulling away from beneath Cion's feet. He squirmed, and in his death rattle he repented of what he had done. I guess it's always like that.

I took the meat down from the wire. Robert took the other end and we carried it into the dining room. That's the lamb done, I thought. Then we went to get Cion. We took him down from the wire to carry him to the dining room. The metal had cut deep into his throat. He had gone to the trouble of binding his feet together; just to make sure, I suppose. He had fastened the wire to the central beam, wrapped the other end around his neck and jumped from a chair. Swinging from left to right, he realised that it was the first time in his life that his feet weren't touching the ground.

Robert took the torso, while I freed the neck. The body slipped from his grasp a little. He staggered as he tried to hold it upright, and then fell onto the bed and ended up in Cion's arms. 'Why does everyone have to die with their eyes open?' Robert asked. He passed his hand over Cion's face to close the swollen eyelids, but they opened again by themselves. I told him it was normal. 'What's normal? You call that normal? Come on, damn it!' Robert said, pacing from wall to wall. I wrapped Cion in a sheet and held him under his arms, and after walking up and down for a minute Robert cooperated and grabbed his heels. No one dared to come out into the corridor, though some timidly held their doors ajar and peered out.

After we had put him down on the table (the meat lay on a chair), Robert took a wet rag back up to the room to erase Cion's last words, written with charcoal on the wall above his bed: 'I'VE LEFT BEFORE YOU AFTER ALL!' The large letters placed the blame for this further death squarely on our shoulders. After that came the digging, just next to Mstislaw's grave. At that moment, the weather changed abruptly: clouds came in from the west, bringing a steady cold rain, like a gift from the mountains. We wrapped Cion in yet another sheet and laid him in ten centimetres of water at the bottom of the pit. A burial in mud. We stood above the grave, and our silence signified our last respects. I looked up into the sky and it began to thunder. Large raindrops lashed my face; thousands of drops. The warm earth began to steam, and curtains of mist rose slowly above the plain. The three-storey, stone building was like a ship lost in the fog.

There was a blackout. Robert went to get a few candles from the kitchen storeroom and we sat on our beds in the flickering candlelight, listening to the rain. Situations like this often reminded Robert of his early childhood, his mother and the snakebite he was proud of. We nibbled pieces of mouldy toast, which we washed down with cold tea. I interrupted Robert while he was describing how he used to get a Coke from the vending machine at the petrol station by inserting fifty cents for two cans of beer so he could stand on them and reach the Coke button. I told him that Mr Smooth had come. He was not surprised. He leafed around in the Bible indifferently, then he walked to the window and looked out into the darkness. 'Next time,' I went, briefly imitating Martin's voice. 'He said that when he comes to see us again we'll definitely be leaving with him. He'll drive,' I added. Instead of an answer there came the harsh sound of paper tearing. Robert was gingerly pulling out pages and releasing them to fly off into the night like doves. Sometimes one would return with a gust of wind and end up on the floor or on my bed. 'And I stood upon the sand of the sea, and saw a beast rise up out of the sea, having seven heads and ten horns, and upon his horns ten crowns, and upon his heads the name of blasphemy.' Robert asked what we would do with the meat. He was still tearing out pages. I wanted to reply with some biblical wisdoms involving lamb, as there are hundreds of them. I perused the torn-out pages: dog, fish, dove... but no mention of lamb. Robert stepped back, took a run-up and flung what was left of the Bible into the thick veil of darkness and rain.

The candles went out. Robert closed the window and sat on his bed again. Now we could hear the sounds coming from within the leprosarium more clearly and heard something more than just the whistle of the wind through the gap beneath the door and the creak of water in the rusty pipes. Robert looked for the matches. A ruddy flash lit up his swollen face.

'Dogs,' he said, 'it's dogs.

A sudden, piercing bark made us start. A rival whined in pain and chairs were being knocked over in the dining room. Hungry jaws pulled the meat apart. They tore off and gulped down large mouthfuls, driven to a frenzy by the taste of the stale lamb's blood. We waited for the menagerie to calm down a little and lit another candle. The sticky sweat on my skin smelt of instinctive fear. It's a different smell from when you sweat from exertion or from the heat – then you smell the dried salt and get the almost pleasant tension on the surface of your skin. Now I licked my right palm, and it was bitter, sour. It was wrinkled, wretched and frightened. Like my life, I thought, and Robert's too. The candles burned down and went out. The rain was easing and we could hear the scrape of dogs' claws on the stone surface of the corridor. I imagined a red tongue dangling. The stench of half-digested meat cascaded over it. An insidious growling approached our door. Dirty canine claws scraped against the old wood. Dogs panted and beat rhythmically with their paws as if they were digging a pit and knew for sure that they would soon be eating two old lepers. We did not budge from our beds but stared in the direction of our would-be killers. I picked up a wrinkled page from the floor and, holding it up to the candle, on my knees, began to read: 'And the beast which I saw was like unto a leopard, and his feet were as the feet of a bear, and his mouth as the mouth of a lion: and the dragon gave him his power, and his seat, and great authority.' I was interrupted by a bark. A long tongue was thrust under the door. The snout beat against the door furiously.

'Keep on reading,' Robert said

'Why?' I asked.

'The grace of God has left this place,' he said.

'No!' I replied, 'It's you and me who should have left this place – long ago.'

Robert grabbed the page angrily, clapping it between his hands to smooth it out, skipped several lines and began to read the passage where God intervenes and crushes the seven-headed beast. He read together with a choir of dogs who, like giant rats, had taken the whole building by storm. There must have been dozens of them. I imagined them nestling up together and warming their shit-soiled bodies. They licked their snouts and enjoyed the safety of the pack. The males were active, and mangy bitches whined as they surrendered to the stabs of thin, red penises. Yellow sperm splashed their insides. Several successful conceptions occurred that evil night.

The rain stopped. There was thunder away in the plain to the east of the leprosarium. The barking had died down and Robert got up and knocked loudly on the door. No answer from the other side: they had probably gone. I said he should go out and check, but he took off his linen robe and crept under the blanket. He needed sleep. He turned over two or three times to find the most comfortable position, gave a deep sigh and wished me good night. His ability to turn off was another of his basic traits conditioned by the years spent in this place. After two or three minutes, I heard the steady breathing and hissing sound of the air passing through his deformed nostrils. The candles were burning the last of their wax and the flames were tall and black at the tips. One went out, leaving a bluish streak of smoke, and then the other died too. A sweetish stench filled the air, intoxicating. I was safe as long as the door was shut, I thought, laying my head on the pillow. Nothing could operate the simple mechanism of the latch, nothing but a human. The animals were hungry, and nature was honed to perfection. Romania was here, and Europe was there, in the direction of my feet. Fear was useful, and the Bible was re-experiencing the Flood in a muddy puddle in the courtyard. I longed to dream of a high-flying flock of pigeons.

I dreamt of Martin. I was riding a green horse, a steed with neatly cut lawn instead of hair. Robert and I were playing golf on that green – we were as small as fleas. The horse's gallop prevented me from taking a proper shot. I aimed at the ball, swung and missed. Everything shook. It was Robert's hand shaking my shoulder. I woke up with the big green horse in my head: a big green headache. Robert had dark rings under his eyes. The window was bathed in light. Several pages of the Bible still stuck to the glass from the outside, like a testament to the preceding night. The tiny letters divided into two columns resembled a huge army as seen from the heavens. The divisions were being arrayed for battle. The page number at the bottom was a mighty general. Robert opened the window and took off the soggy pages. He gave them a shake, laid them out on his bed and tried to read them. Probably he regretted what he had done.

'There are still more under my bed,' I said, looking up at the sky. The sun was smothered by big clouds, dark grey at the edges. Two crows cut across the window. I thought of the green horse again. Nature would soon be getting new colours; the brown hues of the forest and the yellow decay of the useless fields.

When we went down to the dining room and were met by the remains of the bloody feast and the stench of dog excrement. Beside what was left of the lamb's bones there also lay the half-eaten carcass of a dog. Robert said they had perhaps left it in exchange. He reminded me that the Chinese eat dogs. I looked at the spilt entrails and prodded the meat with the tip of my shoe.

'Fresh?' I asked.

'It's just a lamb with long teeth and short wool. Slightly thinner in the thigh and with an angular jaw. The differences are negligible,' Robert said.

For a moment I thought he was being serious and that he would dig into the meat without thinking twice. He watched in silence as I wrapped up the carcass in a large tablecloth. I jabbed the fugitive organs with a fork and returned them to the ragged hole in the belly.

'We'll have to do some more digging,' I told Robert. 'We mustn't leave it out, unburied. The smell will attract even more animals. Who knows what sort,' I said, imagining an Egyptian sphinx stalking the Romanian plain with giant steps.

The dogs kept coming back, but now we firmly closed the ground-floor windows and doors. They ran round and round the building, looking for scraps, and disappeared again before dawn. Robert devoted himself to restoring the Bible. He collected the torn pages, left them to dry and straightened them between layers of cardboard weighed down with bricks. I would go into our room and be met by a mosaic of the First Book of Kings.

'A few more days and the Holy Writ will be one again,' he said, as if wanting to atone for all the sins he had committed and also those that lay ahead. As if he had re-written the book himself. This devotion soothed his conscience. Before going to bed he reviewed the day's work; holding the pages up to the candlelight as if he were searching for hidden meanings inscribed in invisible ink between the lines. He then put the book, buckled like a handful of cabbage leaves, up on the shelf above the bed head and closed his eyes.

Silence descended. Rain drenched the ground day after day, and one day was just like another. The puddles down in the courtyard took on particular shapes and reflected muddy cuttings of the Romanian sky. The factory spewed mouthfuls of black smoke that travelled over the plain like sentinels.

Ceauşescu's portrait now wore a somewhat different smile. As if the corners of his mouth had slipped downwards ever so slightly into sorrow and his overly ruddy cheeks developed a hue of green.

The upshot of the fruitless demonstrations was that five policemen now patrolled the roof of the main factory building day and night, armed to the teeth and shivering with cold. I was not sure whose side I was on. When I thought of the workers I remembered the stones flung at Ingemar Zoltán; at his good intentions and smiling face. The police provoked a different kind of disgust.

One November afternoon I put plastic bags on my feet instead of socks, laced up my shoes very tight, and jumped the fence to go to the rubbish dump. My feet sank into the soggy ground together with the dead grass, and I had to watch carefully where I trod. That is why I didn't notice that one of the five policemen was training his sights on me. When the shot rang out I immediately thought it was the shepherd. I looked all around me, but there were no sheep to be seen. The second shot was accompanied by a sound like a flat stone being flung into soft mud. The bullet hit the ground a few metres in front of me, and its little entry hole smoked and slowly drowned in mud. The policeman was standing at the very corner, facing the plain. He could see me clearly as I took my unsteady steps and raised my arms abruptly to keep my balance on the islands in the boggy ground. When I looked at him he did not take his face away from the sights but waved with the hand that until then had been on the trigger, and then returned it. The small hill of the rubbish dump was now twice as close as the leprosarium behind me, but I decided that if the fool fired again I would run back. If I got pinned down behind the rubbish dump I would have to wait till nightfall to stick my head out again.

The sniper now had an audience. The policemen on the roof gathered round him, and my supporters, the workers, were standing beneath the giant Ceauşescu portrait. Now they were waving too. I felt like an obstinate calf that does not want to move despite all the juicy heads of cabbage being offered to it. In reality it was only my head that was on offer: take it or leave it. If he killed me he would have a simple alibi: a leper stole from the factory, and the policeman diligently discharged his duty.

Slowly I pulled my feet out of the mud. The plastic bags had burst and my toes felt little stones and ooze. I stepped further to the right to try and get to somewhat drier ground. Bang! A whistle above my head. I bent down as if to avoid something else that came with the bullet. I didn't know how fast I could run. I was able to do several hard physical jobs, but running involved continual strain on all muscles, especially those in my legs, which I didn't have faith in. My first step was greeted by ovations from the workers; the second was accompanied by a shot. I wanted the factory's chimney to be the belfry of a cathedral and its clouds of smoke to compose the face of God as I ran with all my might. My knees ached. My lungs became a wrinkled apple and my heart a worm that was burrowing into it. I ran a semicircle around a large puddle topped with the whitish scum of nitrogenous waste. The leprosarium bobbed up and down like a mad thing. Two more shots: one after another. The skin on my face trembled unnaturally whenever my feet touched the ground; I almost felt it would come off.

I was stopped by a powerful blow and great pain. I fell forward into the mud with a splash and waited for the last pangs of consciousness to come; a blessed warmth that would take me away to the hereafter or wherever it is we go. I lay for several more minutes thinking of Robert, then I tried to move my arms and legs.

My ribs hurt. My sight was muddied by pieces of grit that scratched my eyelids from within. I shook myself, trying to get off the Romanian earth, and immediately above my head I recognised the rusty bars of the leprosarium fence hidden in the bushes. So that was the 'weapon' that stopped me!

The black bruise did not come up until the next day. I let Robert put on compresses soaked in some useless herbal infusion. 'Did you see his face?' he asked.

'Whose face?'

'Of the shit who fired,' he said.

'How could I have recognised him at such a distance?'

'I don't know,' Robert shrugged, 'just asking,' and he continued leafing through the Bible. Its pages were now all back together again.

Early that evening the rain turned to sticky snow. Robert had been plagued by a bad cough for several days and was bringing up blood. He had also lost his hearing in his right ear, so when I spoke he turned the left side of his head towards me. And yet another change: instead of the Romanian national anthem, which the factory had blared out at the end of the afternoon shift for years, on 22nd December there came only silence.

CHAPTER NINE

This was not the snow that turns fields and graveyards, meadows and houses into a gentle, picturesque winter landscape; snow that brings a stillness as visible as fog. No, not that snow. Perhaps this impression should be put down to my poor eyesight and my ever worsening mood; but the fact is that as I was shovelling away the piles of white from the stack of firewood next to the chapel, I found creatures in it the size of a child's finger. The snow was full of maggots like rotten meat. Dead snow, I thought; that carpet of dirty white was in fact a huge corpse which would soon exude streams of foulness. Thousands and thousands of maggots were eating away at the ice crystals, and if I listened closely I would probably be able to hear the noise of a million tiny mandibles, and in the silent nights their noise would break like a wave all along the mountain cliffs and reverberate across the whole country. The maggots were eating the fabric of time, I thought.

I threw down the spade and laid the pieces of wet firewood in a bucket. Robert was standing at the window watching the factory yard where an assembly of workers began every morning. During one of these rallies the police went over to the people and were met with thunderous applause. Some of the workers grabbed the policemen's rifles and held an impromptu marksmanship competition, shooting at the face of the dictator, and I realised his time had come. The police grabbed fogged-up bottles of vodka, and all order collapsed. We watched as workers in their overalls loaded office furniture onto sledges pulled by horribly emaciated horses. Instead of thick smoke, the factory's chimney now timidly emitted curls of grey from the almost extinguished machines and ovens. In the office building vandals threw everything out of the windows that was not of use. Piles of account books fell together with the snowflakes and in mid-air turned into flocks of fluttering papers. A tall flame awaited them. Hands were turned towards its warmth. First they settled old accounts with the account books, and then: 'Via Bucureşti!'

The next morning the usual assembly was marked by colourful neo-revolutionary slogans. Two beat-up buses and a number of lorries were waiting to pick up the mass of workers with their flags and banners; after which they would set off for the centre of events. Groups of farmers came across the meadows, and the workers waited for them politely because they were bringing fuel for the revolution: large quantities of home-made brandy to prepare empty stomachs and empty heads for the great cause.

The motors coughed into life. The procession set off to win freedom. Robert and I stood in the bushes near the fence waiting for the masses to pass the curve closest to the leprosarium. They looked pretty miserable. I now realised how two or three decrepit old vehicles could carry such a seemingly impressive load. I had never seen so many emaciated people all together. In one of the buses the protesters smashed most of the windows and stuck out long poles with flags and banners. Whenever a wheel hit a pothole, everyone inside hopped and bobbed in unison. The last lorry which lagged behind the others and belched black smoke was for the women. They shrieked a lively folksong and our eardrums quivered painfully as they passed.

Lonely tractors crawled across the surrounding meadows and fields, loaded with new groups of malcontents. The snow began to fall more heavily. The flakes were finer and came in thicker swirls. All things that moved on the plain slowly disappeared under a mantle of white as if a huge cataract was descending veil-like from the sky and dimming the world. It was obvious that something important was going to happen there, on the city streets. I felt an urge to walk off into that white: to jump the fence, pull my hood over my head and set off on a roadless journey, embracing the vastness of the landscape. It would be a long walk. I would meet animals, trees and hillocks. In the end I would have to meet people too; their horrified eyes, their hands ready to throw stones, their mouths pursed to swear. I caressed the ice-clad fence and pressed my cold palm against my tired eyelids.

Robert suggested we go back to the room. He waved his hand in front of his nose, driving away swarms of snowflakes. He picked up several frozen pieces of firewood, coughed to clear his throat and spat out a red spot into the snow. His face was a yellowish hue. The wrinkles stood out more than usual, and the skin on his forehead had contracted into six folds. I instinctively felt my own forehead and counted four, and for the first time I thought how our convincing slow, compelling disease had rendered us oblivious to the signs of time slowly wrapping us in the cobweb of age. I took one more look at Robert before he went in through the dark frame of the door: his stumbling gait and his back bent under such a small load. Striding out into the ever thicker snow, I felt something important had to happen which we would both remember as we counted our last days.

The wet wood hissed in the fire like a cornered rat and I fed it a handful of dried elm bark. Heating the high-walled room was not easy and we needed to go easy on the wood. If the workers did not come the next day, I would try to get some coal from the factory's boiler-room. Probably only small fragments were left, as all the good stuff was carried away that afternoon in big sacks. To keep himself warm, Robert collected the blankets from the now uninhabited rooms. I declined when he offered me one because I did not know which had been Kasiewicz's. Anyway, Robert needed the blankets much more than I did. His cough kept me awake until the early hours. The night before, I had also been unable to get to sleep because of the clattering of a helicopter that circled low over the factory and the nearby villages. Beams of light scribbled on the snow as it searched roads and fields. As it was flying along above the highway, tracer bullets were fired at it, and the giant insect returned the fire. They were too far away for me to hear the gunfire properly. With a bit of fantasy I could imagine the whole world being occupied by insects the size of helicopters. Airborne guards patrolled the skies above a subjugated humanity and punished any attempt at revolution. Children looked up into the black-spotted skies with fear. Mothers cried, knowing that their offspring would become either prey or slaves. I knew that even in a world like that I would be where I was now. I would dream the same dreams and speak the same words. I would remain a leper.

I was woken by the cold. It pinched my ears and nose. I had fallen asleep without the blankets over me, and now I felt icicles wedged in my joints. I thought of red-hot coals, the petrified warmth of prehistoric plants, and went to the window to see what was happening at the factory. Snow was still clinging to large depressions in Ceaușescu's face, looking just like giant dollops of guano. A fire was burning brightly in the sheltered part of the yard and several people in green army uniforms were sitting round it. They were unarmed. One of them, draped in a long overcoat, walked to the corner every five minutes to look out over the plain. I went back to bed, wrapped myself in the blankets and tried to go to sleep.

When I was woken from my half-sleep by gunfire I thought to myself that I had never been woken in the leprosarium by a normal noise like the crowing of a rooster or the banging of a window in the wind. It was always Robert's loud cough, the barking of dogs or the bellowing of the other residents; or at best a nightmare or the ringing of the rocket, neither of which can exactly be described as normal. I sprang to the window again. Twenty or so policemen had surrounded the factory: concealing themselves behind piles of rubbish, they trained their rifles. No one was left by the fire any more. One of the men lay in the snow. If I had approached, I would probably have seen a red river of blood flowing from beneath the body like a mountain stream. I would see it babble through a small canyon and sink into the snow. Three green uniforms and one arm with a pistol stuck out of a window on the second floor. The man was saving his bullets, so he responded to the loud bursts of fire from the ground with just one or two shots. A policeman under cover of the storage shed pointed to show the others the location of a small side entrance. They showered the building with several intensive salvoes and charged at the dark opening in the wall.

After ten minutes of explosions and shouting, a man in green uniform jumped from the platform above the storage shed. He had run around the edge of the roof, probably looking for stairs down. I assume he heard the stamp of boots on the metal rungs and instinctively made the futile further step of climbing up to the large water tank. He was still a step ahead of his pursuers, when a rifle protruded from an open door, then behind it another, and then yet another even longer one. The man slowly put down his gun, went up to the edge of the roof and spread his arms, turning the heavy green overcoat into a large cape with shiny black lining. The cape fluttered as the man fell through the air. He jumped without thinking twice, as if he were convinced he would fly and make it to heaven. The policemen ran up to the edge. I did not see if the fallen body moved or not, but one of them aimed and fired a shot which put an end to any movements there might have been. Then the policemen went back inside the building and no more shots were fired until they brought out two more soldiers at gunpoint; also apparent Ceauşescu loyalists. The policemen forced them to take off their uniforms and ordered them to run away across the fields. They let them get a little distance, just enough for them to think their captors would not shoot and that the forest was closer than it looked. A policeman took off his cap and aimed. The naked bodies collapsed into the snow. The man who had fired walked up to them and slowly drew his pistol from the leather holster at his side. Two bullets for two heads: certain death, and chubby worms rushed to feed on the lukewarm blood.

Three more corpses were then dragged out of the building. The blue-uniformed men leaned their rifles up against the wall and laid the dead under Ceauşescu's face. Their hands now greedily took the bottle of vodka, and their mouths drank deeply, taking the edge off the horror and allowing the killers to feel alright again. Quite alright. They waited by the fire and then, with the help of the driver who came up and shook hands with them all, they threw the bodies in through the rear door of his van. A quarrel broke out. The driver checked the tyres and shook his head: he could not drive through the snow with a load like that. He could only take four corpses. His yellow glove seized the bare foot that was sticking out and pulled. A policeman threw down his rifle, rolled up his sleeves and dumped the naked man back in with the other corpses. He slammed the rear door and brushed his hands clean. The driver reached for the door handle again but was met by the butt of a Kalashnikov and several blows from a truncheon.

Robert's cough woke him up and he found himself lying on his side. He rubbed his eyes and tried to see what the time was. I told him to stay in bed until I had lit the stove and he pointed to something below his bed, where half-dried lumps of blood and yellowish mucous covered the bottom of the metal basin. He cleared his throat again and added a large lump of the same colour to the slurry. I said I would go and make some tea, but Robert just shook his head and took the Bible down from the shelf above his bed. He pressed it against his sweaty chest as if trying to exorcise the demon dwelling there.

Outside the factory the van tried to start. The policemen pushed, closing their eyes and mouths to avoid the thick mud being kicked up by the wheels. When the tyres finally encountered firm ground and the vehicle spat out several clouds of smoke, one of the blue-uniformed men fired his gun into the air to let off steam. Their car beside the factory road bore a Romanian flag with a hole where the red star used to be. History would probably call people like this 'dogs of the revolution', I thought, and gaped at Robert, who was about to spit out another piece of his lungs. He asked if Martin had come. The faded four-wheel-drive with the four corpses disappeared behind the birches. I decided not to tell Robert what I had seen that morning, as it would only upset him further.

I had difficulty imagining which side Martin would take. I could see him equally well among the demonstrators, who went with the flow for the sake of their own future and took no big risks, and the faithful old guard of the toppled dictator, who defended the empire to the last bullet.

A kind of anarchy reigned in the country. Columns of black smoke rose from the direction of the E79 highway like leeches sucking the sky, like Towers of Babel turned upside down. Christmas was coming and I hoped it would be sunny. I thought all these things as I carried a wooden tray with a jug of hot tea and two greasy glasses up to the room. As I walked past the doors on the way to ours I listened to see if there was any noise or coherent speech. For several days now the leprosarium had been much too quiet, I thought, and kicked open one of the wobbly wooden doors. The window in the room was open and my face struck a wall of cold and several snowflakes. I knew I would not find anyone. I knew there was no one else in the room next door, nor in the one next to it, nor in the whole building. They had left that windless night, accompanied by muffled barking. Robert had asked me what was happening, and I had answered that it was just the dogs. But the rusks were gone from the kitchen the next day. Snow had covered their tracks during the night so it was impossible to tell which way they had gone, yet still I wandered around the fence searching for a sign. Robert came out, walking in my footsteps. I thought he wanted to say something, to comment on the exodus, but he only tugged at my elbow and said, 'We need to get some more wood, the cold is unbearable.' That day his cough turned into a beastly rumble.

The first workers arrived at noon. They cleaned up the factory yard and burned all the refuse from the revolution. A little later only the upper half of Ceauşescu's face was leering down from the wall and after a break for lunch and vodka the rest was whitewashed. The landscape seemed very different now. After you have looked at a large black head on the horizon for years and years, it becomes an inseparable part of your everyday picture of the world, especially if it grins stupidly at that world from the same spot every day.

Robert fell asleep, allowing me some peace and quiet. I watched the gathering crowd of people confused by the abrupt changes. They stopped near the white wall pockmarked by gunfire as if wondering whose head would be painted there next. It would have been an ideal spot for a stylised crucifixion topped by a rainbow, I thought, but I was unable to think of so many pretty colours all at once.

Later that day an expensive black limousine drove up. The new post-revolutionary director, accompanied by two police officers, inspected the entire building and called the workers together in the storage shed. Half an hour later everyone came out wildly gesticulating. I assume they were euphorically discussing the most striking parts of a speech that had convinced them that a better future had arrived; that it was not somewhere far away but here and now. The factory's rubbish dump was supplemented with large pieces of broken glass, a product of the euphoria of the first hours of the new era. The loudspeakers reverberated to *Deşteaptă-te, Române*, 'Romania Awake', and the workers in their blue overalls gave the V-for-victory sign in response as they entered the factory. The tower of bricks soon began to spout smoke, the director waved to the workers from the roof, and Robert coughed as if he were being choked by precisely that same smoke.

I sat on my bed, trying to deceive my hunger by chewing soft little pieces of elm bark from the bottom of the cup. There was no flame in the stove, only a heap of cold ash. I scooped up a handful of it and let it trickle between my fingers. Thousands of tiny grey particles, snow made by the hand of a little god, covered the floorboards, raining down on Robert's sleeping head, the Bible and the tips of my shoes.

Ash is an ominous substance, I thought, blowing gently to try and get it off Robert. I knelt down on the floor, pursed my lips and blew hard, trying to drive the heap away. But whenever I blew the dust under the bed, finely shredded pieces of Europe emerged from that forgotten darkness. The remains of the map flew up like frightened butterflies. Pieces of Brittany, Lisbon, Moscow, the wilds of central Spain, several Croatian islands; white-capped mountains, expanses of green and lakes I did not recognise. The factory loudspeakers still blared 'Romania Awake', but I was unable to find that extolled piece of earth. I gathered the remaining paper, adding two or three of Robert's statistical yearbooks and an old Medical Gazette, and lit the stove. It burned with the green flame of printer's ink and gradually gave off a hint of heat. After warming my ribs, I wrapped myself up tightly in a blanket to try and keep that pleasant gooseflesh for as long as possible.

Soon ice covered the windows again. The revolutionary ballad began to skip and was replaced by the enraptured shrieking of women with folk instruments in the background. I imagined glowing faces framed in embroidered kerchiefs. Women like that usually have moustaches, those disgusting little brown hairs; enough to make you forget the shining eyes, firm breasts and the bundle of perfumed hair. Beauty is definitely in the eye of the beholder, I thought, and let my eyelids fall shut.

From the distance, came the rumble of a heavy lorry, like the coughing of giants, or perhaps the destruction of the Berlin Wall or some other bastion. It seemed as if there was a loud combustion of diesel fuel right under our window or somewhere very close by. I got up and scraped at the ice that had taken hold from the inside as well. The crystal shapes glistened, lit up by the sad eyes that trembled beyond the gate. With a little fantasy I could imagine a large mechanical dog delivering the final blows to our fortress of suffering. Its jaws tore down the metal fence as if it were made of sticks. Its steel paws made the ground shake. The dry skulls of Cion Eminescu, Mstislaw Kasiewicz and Margareta Yosipovich shuddered in their graves condemned to oblivion; the anonymous bones of lepers in the nearby fields clattered in fear.

I opened the window. There was less noise than I had imagined. The years of silence had made my sense of hearing hypersensitive. The lorry sounded its horn several times, then put the pedal to the metal and moved forwards. The fence slowly bent. Metal bars whined on both sides of the gate as they were pushed to the ground. There was a moment of extreme tension and everything began to break. The large wheels pressed the iron into the snow. I woke Robert, and he woke his cough. He struggled to the window and roared even louder. His lungs were irritated by the cold air mixed with exhaust gases.

The lorry stopped next to the fountain. The violet lights of the factory bit into the twilight.

The lorry door clacked and the motor fell silent. Martin jumped out into the snow. He brought a Kalashnikov and a metal fuel canister from the cabin, stopped beneath our window and laid the things in the snow.

'Gentlemen, your passports please!' he called out with a military salute.

Robert's legs could not take the excitement – he sat by the stove, holding his knees and staring at a spot on the floor. I returned Martin's salute and ran downstairs. Instead of an elegant leather jacket he was wearing an ordinary blue police uniform with several golden stars on the lapel. It seemed he had taken sides. I went up to embrace him, but he stepped back and stopped me with his hand in a rubber glove.

'Sorry, I forgot,' I said.

Martin called me to the back of the lorry. He raised the tarpaulin and lifted out a large sack with the emblem of the postal service. I took a second one. They were bulging and soft. We took them and put them on the table in the dining room. He asked me to get Robert and then lit a cigarette.

I had begun to feel that stupid nostalgia already. It was a conspiracy of habit, I supposed. When the last Chinese emperor was freed of the ritual fetters that he had borne until adolescence, as the laws of his dynasty prescribed, he periodically asked for them to be put back on because they had become a natural part of his world-view and his body.

The legend has it that he would stroll through the spacious squares of the Forbidden City and enjoy the clatter of his heavy chains as if it were the song of the black nightingale. I felt something similar. Despite all my happiness at finally leaving, as I went up to get Robert, I ran my hand gently over the grimy walls of that accursed house. Even stranger: my eyes filled with tears and butterflies began to flutter in my stomach: those too familiar butterflies.

Robert now stood in the middle of the room. When he saw me he wiped his tears on his sleeve and beamed. We hugged each other tight, and with my arms still around him, I managed to lift him and carry him out. Yet he still went back to look at the room one last time. He took the Bible and closed the window. 'So it won't be too cold if we return,' he said.

I took my passport out of the drawer, grabbed several other small objects and my birthday presents, then took Robert by the arm and turned out the light. We stood in the corridor and looked into the darkness of our room. As I closed the door, I thought that if I were to take a memento that would condense all that I had been through and thought about in this room over all the long years, it would be a slice of that thick, damp darkness. I had the feeling that something had finished and something else was now beginning. The greasy light bulbs along the corridor bid us farewell us with a flicker caused by the varying voltage. I didn't dare turn round for fear there might be more than just a section of shabby floor in the dank air and yellowish light; perhaps I would see of the faces of the former residents, disfigured by suffering and disease, or even the lost souls of dead lepers. Robert was staggering because of his cough, so I quickened my step and helped him along.

Martin was emptying the sacks onto the table. A cigarette smouldered in the left corner of his mouth and he squinted to avoid the smoke. It was hard to imagine what a huge pile could come out of five postal sacks. In spite of my impaired sense of smell I detected a pleasant whiff of perfume. I moved closer and took a deep breath in order to fill my lungs with the sweetish odour. A heap of clothes lay on the table: expensive Italian suits, shirts and silk waistcoats. The sleeve of a dress uniform edged with gold braid was sticking out, and a trouser leg hung down over the edge showing its red velvet hem. Martin instructed us to take whatever we liked.

Fine cotton is soothing for the skin, and the heavy trousers of triple-spun wool made me feel warmer straight away. Robert enthusiastically donned a pair of Levi Strauss denims and let out some juicy American swear words. I also threw him a polo-neck jumper which he put on over pyjamas with stylised initials. Martin watched us from the corner and looked at his watch from time to time. After we had put on as many clothes as we could, including two or three pairs of socks each, we measured each other to gauge the effect. Our crafted heads protruded from the beautiful colours and sumptuous textiles like unnatural and crooked extensions. Martin rummaged around and finally found two warm woollen caps which we pulled down over our foreheads almost to our eyes. He asked to see our passports. Robert's was still out in the hole in the wall, so I went to retrieve it. I threw the stone into the snow and trembled with fear when I heard barking behind the fence. Then I reached in my hand and took the green booklet. I didn't put the piece of masonry back in its place and I wondered if I would later come to think of the leprosarium as an injured patient left to bleed to death.

Back in the dining room I was met by the sharp smell of petrol; Martin was walking around with the canister, pouring fuel on the clothes on the table as well as the wooden chairs and the kitchen fittings. When the canister was empty he threw it on the floor. I handed him the passport, which he now put it in the pocket of his military blouse. He sat down and lit a cigarette, and carefully extinguished the match between his fingers. He signalled that we should go out, took a last few drags on his cigarette and then came after us. We stood in front of the main door, waiting for the moment when the whole building would become a mighty torch devouring the dark. The wooden floors and beams would catch fire quickly and the blaze would soon spread to the attic and roof, the old furniture, the mattresses and the wool-filled pillows.

Martin positioned his cigarette butt between his index finger and his thumb, then glanced at us with a smile as if he wanted our support in what he was about to do.

Flick. The glowing red point landed on the floorboards. There was a flame, first green, then changing to orange, which climbed up the table leg, engulfed the sleeve of the uniform and spread irreversibly. We withdrew towards the lorry. The heat was already radiating out into the snow. Plates broke and wood screeched. Martin went up to the door, which was being licked by long tongues of fire. He flung something into the jaws of the fire, and before I could even cry out I realised they were not birds or anything else, but our passports. They burst into flames like two feathers and became part of the inferno. 'Jesus Fucking Christ!' cried Robert; I picked up the Kalashnikov out of the snow, released the safety catch and pointed it at Martin, who slowly raised his hands. If I had killed him, it would have been from pent-up rage from putting up with all the horrible humiliations of the disease. My finger trembled on the trigger, waiting for the signal to squeeze. I thought of Kasiewicz; buried, I knew now, because of a worthless wad of paper. It took me twenty seconds to empty the whole magazine. I fired at the blaze through the windows on the ground floor; I shattered several first-floor windows, as well as that of our room. Heavy pieces of tile began to fall from the roof.

Martin said I was a fool and snatched the Kalashnikov from my hands. He jumped into the cabin, started the motor, and pointed for us to get in the back. He swore in Romanian as he stepped on the gas and made three or four half-turns trying to reach the gate. The tyres screeched and showered snow. Yes, the burnt passports were worthless wads of paper, and the stamps and signatures of the former Securitate agents that authorised them were now void. If Martin had said this on time I would not have fired; and we would not now have been banging our heads against the bars, trying to catch one last glimpse of our old home through the branches of the birches. Now we had to vanish before the workers, alarmed by the shooting, came out into the factory yard and ran to the leprosarium with buckets of water. By the time we reached the main road, the flames had already broken through the roof. The beams collapsed, leaving only the thick walls illuminated with an apricot colour. The screaming skull of Europe's last leprosarium disappeared in the embrace of a fiery medusa. Somehow I was glad I would remember it like this: a dignified old creature, majestic in its fall.

CHAPTER TEN

*'Deşteaptă-te, române, din somnul cel de moarte, / În care te-adânciră barbarii de tirani! /
Acum ori niciodată croieşte-ţi altă soarte, / La care să se-nchine şi cruzii tăi duşmani.'*

'Awake, Romania, from your deathly sleep/Into which the barbaric tyrants have made you sink/Now, or never, your fate renew/And watch your enemies bow before you'.

Whenever we drove up to patrols of self-appointed militiamen and Martin showed them his documents, making them lower their hunting rifles again with an expression of respect and fraternal solidarity, this melody resounded from the lorry's radio. It seemed to me that everything that was happening in the country originated from that one song; that it must contain secret codes directed at the brain centres that control the creation of revolutions. The patrol would hand Martin a bottle of home-made brandy or vodka, he would take a swig, give the V-for-victory sign and continue driving, humming to rouse the sleepy nation as we went.

We left the asphalt for a tangle of poor, unsealed roads which also had their share of patrols. The bumpy tracks were blocked in places by logs, and these checkpoints would usually be manned by peasants, brown up to their knees in cow-dung: supernumeraries with pitchforks and other rural props who had been given a role in the last European revolution. Martin would screech to a halt, sending a slurry of snow and mud to rain down on the curious women and sleepy children huddled around the fire. He blew the horn continuously and held the red booklet up against the windscreen until two men lifted the log and made the road passable.

Martin turned off into a cornfield to pour in some more fuel. He lifted the flap of the tarpaulin, released the metal bolt and called us to get out.

The snow cover on the ground was thin and we left black footprints wherever we trod. The plain was dark and still. A yellowish glow faintly lit up the clouds in the distance, and Martin said those were the lights of Bucharest. He finished refuelling and threw away the canister, telling us he'd like to have a cigarette here in the open, if we weren't too cold. It wasn't cold, I said, cotton kept you nice and warm. Martin came up and straightened my collar, which had been sticking out. He felt the material and was visibly impressed by the quality. 'He wore only the best,' he said.

'Who is He?' I asked.

'Dra-cu-la!' pronounced Martin and widened his eyes to conjure up the horror that belonged to that name. I knew he did not mean Vlad the Impaler but the common nickname for their dictator. I looked closely at Robert's chest, turned down the neck of the jumper and tried to read the initials embroidered on the pyjamas. A stylised 'C' embraced a stylised 'N', and I realised that our warm new clothes came from the wardrobe of Nicolae Ceauşescu.

Martin laughed when I lifted up my arm and sniffed the armpit. There was a sweetish odour of sweat, and that sweat meant history. Robert did the same, but his nose was unable to detect any historical anomalies.

We continued on our way, sniffing the clothing from time to time. We bumped up and down along a gravel road, avoiding potholes full of slushy snow. When Robert wanted to spit out a chunk of his sickly lungs, I knocked on the glass of the cabin and Martin slowed down. Then Robert leaned out the back and gave Romania what it deserved. We stopped again just before dawn: at the horizon a long yellow line of approaching light was dividing the darkness. Between the branches we heard a slow rumble like the rolling of a gigantic wave: the voice of the Danube hidden behind a dense thicket of willows. The thought of defying that power and travelling upstream through the heart of the continent horrified me as much as the realisation that we were in fact to travel without a goal, borne by an ill-defined desire for change, movement and meaning. For a moment I was prepared to return to the smoking ruins of the leprosarium, put the missing stone back in the wall and resurrect my miserable life there.

Branches scratched my hands and face, opening half-healed wounds. I feared that Robert wouldn't make it. I put my arm around his shoulders; he was shaking. Fever had him in its grips again. His feet sank ever deeper into the mud. With effort he lifted his shoes and shook off the thick clumps of red earth. And then finally we reached our goal: the seething surface of the water with a veil of morning mist levitating above it. The far bank was still invisible, so it was as if we were standing on the edge of a huge maelstrom. Carefully, Martin trod out onto the wooden ferry landing, glancing up and downriver on the lookout for Romanian border police. When he was satisfied that the river was deserted, he called for us to come. He was still smoking and kept looking at his watch. 'They should be here any time now', he said, throwing his cigarette butt into the water. We sat down on the damp boards and looked into the river, which made us dizzy. Plastic Coca-Cola bottles emptied at the Vienna docks, small gas cylinders, light bulbs and pieces of polystyrene bobbed along like shipwrecked souls caught in the current. Sunken branches snagged torn plastic bags; a technocrat's harvest that shone in many colours. While Robert and I watched the slow dawn, Martin lit a fire on the bank. He broke off dead branches, collected bundles of reeds and made a pyramid of them on a tree stump. A flock of crows attracted by the smoke landed in the nearby thicket. I helped Robert get up. His hands were icy cold, and we went close to warm ourselves.

Martin rubbed his hands and jumped up and down. It was one of those moments when reality resembles a damaged record that skips and repeats the same sequence without end. I shifted the needle and asked him what had happened to the group that left the leprosarium earlier. '*Sis mortuus mundo, vivus iterum Deo*,' (Dead be thou to the world, but living anew to God), he replied, still hopping up and down. 'They wandered off westwards. The cold decimated them. Those that survived made it to an old railway line that leads to a coal mine in the foothills. There they found an abandoned house by the track. They'll die of hunger, the fools. The country is in anarchy, and every revolution, unfortunately, separates the wheat from the chaff. There's no hope for them, I'm afraid.'

'Dead to the world, but living anew to God,' I echoed. 'Won't it be the same with us?'

Martin was silent, and added some more dry branches to the fire without making a reply. What could he have said anyway? Robert crossed himself and stared into the flames.

Unlike today, the excommunication of lepers in the past was at least rich in ritual. The quarantined leper would be taken to the church, laid like a corpse on a wooden stretcher and covered with a black sheet. The priest would sing the responsorial Libera Me. The black mass would be said, and the unfortunate individual taken away to the leprosarium. If such an institution did not exist, a hut with four black-locust posts would be built twenty feet from the road. The leper survived thanks to the alms that kind-hearted travellers threw to the hovel. When the leper died, the hut was cremated together with the corpse. In a different version, the leper was borne out of the House of God and to the graveyard. To symbolically illustrate the exclusion from the world of the healthy, they lowered the leper into a freshly dug grave. The priest would lay a clod of earth on their head and say: 'My friend, this is a sign that you are dead to the world, but that you are living in God.' Then they would be taken away to the leprosarium on a stretcher with iron hooks. The leper died a slow death, awaiting the call to the place where there is no illness, where all are clean and white, without stench or stain – more radiant than the sun.

The birds took flight without warning, leaving several grey feathers in the air to waft down to the snow. Quickly, Martin scooped together a pile of wet soil and dumped it on the fire. We withdrew into the bushes, while he cocked his Kalashnikov and kneeled by the landing. We heard questions shouted on board a boat and the muffled answers of the mechanic. Martin signalled for us to keep quiet. He waddled to a nearby bush and positioned his gun between its forked branches.

I did not know what language they were speaking. The fog softened the vowels, and despite the volume of the voices all we heard was a cottony echo. The first thing we saw was a large Soviet flag painted beneath the bow, then after it came a black hull with the red letters LENINGRAD.

Martin gradually got up. He put down his gun, ran out onto the landing and yelled the code word which sounded like the name of some slimy Russian dish. The answer from the deck was in the same tone. This was our boat then – a long flat barge that rose just two or three metres out of the water. When it was quite close, I saw two black figures unwinding ropes at the bow. One swung his arm and a long soggy snake began to squirm on the foot boards. Our guide grabbed the end and fastened the rope to the pier. The turning of a heavy toothed wheel could be heard. An iron gangway lowered itself from the deck onto the boards like the arm of a dying colossus. The crash almost threw Martin off balance. He grabbed the thick rope just in time and jumped onto the rungs of the gangway that led straight to the black hull and the flag. His unsteady feet tested every step. A call of encouragement came through the fog: everything was made of steel, it said – Russian steel. They met half way: a formal handshake and short conversation. The captain pointed to the barge and Martin towards us. Robert began to cough as if he wanted to draw attention to our existence. Mr Smooth reached his hand into his inside pocket. The Russian took off his beret, put it under his arm and accepted a bundle of banknotes. He licked the tips of his fingers, counted the money twice, then returned the beret to his bald head and walked back on deck. Mr Smooth looked to the left and then to the right, downriver. He walked back down to the wooden landing and called for us to come. I felt cold sweat on my neck. Robert stared at the thin streaks of smoke rising from the extinguished fire. 'Are we going?' I asked, but he still gazed at the glowing willow embers.

Spreading the wet soil, I packed on a handful of mud to completely smother the fire. Only then did he try to stand up, holding on to the rotten stump. The Russian waved nervously, trying to get us to hurry, but Robert was now dumbfounded and looked up at the sky with wide eyes and at the tall trees that held him up. His indecision was not caused by his physical discomforts, or by the fever or pain in the lungs. Robert W. Duncan was fighting against a powerful, unrestrainable tide of reflection on what had become of his life. He groaned, caught up in the same ghastly thoughts that befall people who commit suicide, prisoners on death row or women who have just had a stillbirth. The whites of his eyes reflected the pearly shine of the winter landscape. He gazed all around, refusing to blink, as if the tiny curtains that were his eyelids, the movement of minuscule muscles in the corner of his eyes, would destroy not only the existing world but the one that had been and the one that was to come. Robert had to blink several times, in quick succession. I grabbed him firmly by the forearm and pulled him away. I wanted to rip him away from that intensifying mental maelstrom. He stared at me and then at the barge. Floating branches banged into its bow and then sank among the whirlpools of the swollen river. 'Come on, let's go,' I said.

The Russian waved nervously with both arms, and Martin tried to calm him with some hushed words. When Robert finally held onto my shoulder and began to move his feet, Martin and the Russian fell silent and each moved to opposite sides of the gangway. Martin took off his cap and wiped the sweat from his forehead. Then he put the cap under his arm, took out a rubber glove from his inside pocket and put it on his right hand. I stood as straight as I could and quickly tidied up my clothes to suit the solemn mood of the moment. The mechanic turned on the engine. The vibrations spread to the gangway, making the tiny stones and lumps of mud on the edge slip quavering into the river. The Russian stepped back and theatrically removed his beret as if we were a deposed royal couple secretly fleeing the country after a revolution. I shook Martin's glove. And he shook my hand, fidgeting as he stood. 'Save yourselves,' he said, looking me in the eyes. I tried to smile.

Just then Robert coughed. Martin stepped back a few feet. The barge's engine coughed and spluttered even louder. Robert's hand shook and squeezed the rusty cords of the railing. 'Come on boys, there's a long trip ahead!' the Russian said, as he clapped his hands and ran up the gangway. 'Off we go!' he yelled, happily fondling the bundle of banknotes in his inside pocket.

I could not find the words to say goodbye. Instinctively I raised my right hand and gave a military salute, standing at attention. Martin did the same, and I thought I saw two crystal tears in the corners of his eyes. 'Go west,' he called, 'Good luck!'

It felt as though I hadn't heard anyone say that for a long time.

The gangway was lifted to the noises of a heavy winch. A faint shudder ran through the metal colossus, the engine howled and there was a velvety splash of cold water, then the barge started moving and the landscape began to rock. We were standing on a deck covered in patches with shiny scales. The smell of fish mingled with the heavy odour of

Russian oil. Robert leaned over, gagged, and from his mouth gushed a greenish river of half-digested food. After emptying his stomach he wiped his mouth on his sleeve and sighed deeply. He gathered the remains of the acidic substance and spat towards the shore. Martin disappeared among the bushes, the Russian vanished below deck.

He and the mechanic, as it turned out, were preparing our apartment. In fact he called it a hole, and that's what it was it. We were to savour its comforts all the way to the edge of Western Europe, to the deserted Vienna docklands, the heart of darkness, where two lepers' waves of hope would break against the cyclopean wall of a different world. 'Your Honour,' the Russian said, fingering the large-bore Zbrojovka pistol beneath his belt, 'everything is ready. This way, please.'

A spiral staircase wound down into the darkness beneath the stern. After his high fever and vomiting, Robert was hardly able to move his feet down the triple spiral and we felt our way down using the floor and the steel wall. On one side there were two small round portholes about the diameter of teacups – two holes that would show us foggy pictures of the riverbank, the patrol boats of various armies, and the silhouettes of cities: more magnificent and beautiful the farther we travelled west. The iron door closed with a creak and finally with a crash with which the whole lower deck resounded.

This was the first take of a film whose plot no one knew, least of all us two, I thought as I lowered Robert onto the greasy, oil-smeared blanket. He leaned his back against the metal wall between us and the engine room. It ensured us a source of warmth that would save us from freezing in the next four days. It also ensured a tormenting noise that would stop us from sleeping. The whine of the pistons hindered any form of communication, whereas not long before, soft words had rung out clearly in the cold, high-ceilinged rooms of the leprosarium.

Reading words from Robert's leprosy-maimed lips was impossible, and he was hardly able to move his hands. He would stare up at the little portholes, waiting for me to catch sight of a city with my healthy right eye and to write on the metal wall with a finger dipped in a little puddle of oil: MĂGURELE, CALAFAT, BEOGRAD, then VUKOVAR, MOHÁCS, DUNAFÖLDVÁR, BUDAPEST, and later ESZTERGOM, KOMÁRNO, BRATISLAVA, and finally WIEN. Vienna! My finger wrote with a broad trail. My eye followed the green signs with the names of the cities on the Danube whose lights rose above the weeds and dilapidated harbour warehouses all white with hoarfrost.

The little vent at the bottom of our door was opened once a day. A gnarled Russian hand would stick through to take back the empty bowl and return it full of a soupy mixture with pieces of half-cooked fish. I set the fish aside for Robert and piled the bones in the corner. The little heap grew, forming a pyramid of spines and ribs, a transient monument to insignificant deaths, a fragile symbol of our presence here and our journey into the heart. 'The heart of darkness', I said out loud, but my voice was silenced by the whine of the engine. I thought of the hordes of wild Slavic tribes prowling the banks and rattling their weapons. So it once was, and so it would be again, I imagined.

In the year of our lord 1487, victorious Ferdinand, King of Aragon, took Isabella, Queen of Castille to be his wife, and the two mighty Pyrenean kingdoms were finally united beneath one bloody crown.

The celebrations, which the legends say lasted seventy-three days, shook the spires of the Moorish mosques; from his minaret, the muezzin no longer saw peaceful streets but hordes of terrified women and small children; horses' hooves clattered past as Arab knights headed for the final battle; knights whose heads would soon roll on the pavements of Ayerbe, Zaragoza and Pamplona. A world was overturned, its fragrant gardens trampled, Mohammed's words reduced to dust, the fountains laid dry yet drenched with young blood.

Ferdinand and beautiful Isabella knew that the downfall of the great enemy would play into the hands of small enemies and that many wise men of the unified kingdom desired to become sultan in place of the sultan. The whims of battle-proven fighters who had charged the Arab scimitars received satisfaction in the sumptuous uniforms of the new crown and titles of royal counsel; arrogant aristocrats were pacified by regular banquets, drinking parties and damsels to deflower in the sheltered chambers of the court. These cries of lust were mingled with screams of pain from the damp cellars of the palace where all the Moorish secrets were to be plucked out, all the Moorish treasures dug up. The walls were set with chains, the cells equipped with the evil devices of cunning mechanics; yet the most secret room lay at the lowest level of the southern wing of the catacombs, furnished with a luxury worthy of royal chambers, precious canopies, rosewood intarsias and a gilded statuette of the Virgin Mary. A carpet of black wool, crystal glasses and silver candlesticks awaited their guest, arousing the curiosity of the guards and court retinue.

A rainy November night howling with icy mountain winds was good cover for the coach drawn by the horses of the royal guard. The fortress quickly swallowed the unusual procession, and the guards saw to it that the gate was closed almost noiselessly. The guest arrived, it was rumoured, in the company of his bride. Sheltered by the shields of the queen's most loyal officers, the couple took up their abode in the scented living quarters in the cellar, lit by only one torch. For days no inquisitive eyes were able to peer past the muscular chests of the well-armed guards. Since the anniversary celebration of the union of the two kingdoms was approaching, the mysterious guests garnered less and less curiosity and in the end were completely forgotten. Except perhaps for a faint trace of malicious satisfaction on the queen's tender lips when she returned from nightly visits to the damp basement rooms.

The celebrations were as befitted a powerful young dynasty – the best Sicilian wine flowed in rivers and the table was replete with all manner of exotic game. The masses shrieked in delight beneath the walls as they were showered with roast pheasant and young goat's thighs cooked in milk. All received equal satisfaction and left the citadel with full stomachs and bolstered egos, digesting the royal honour they had been accorded and which they would later recall in tales told to their children, grandchildren and servants. But not everyone would tell those tales.

Only a select few, hand-picked by the queen, had the honour of attending her banquet in the highest tower and to be presented in person to the envoys of distant lands who shook hands with everyone in turn. The last couple, falsely announced as Prince Eugene the Younger, Lord of Oltenia, and his wife Constanta, did not deign to smile at the other guests. Their faces were concealed by mother-of-pearl masks in which only their eyes could be seen. Before bowing and shaking hands, the couple, contrary to the custom, removed their silken gloves, and the guests interpreted this as a sign of particular consideration and did the same. He who had rough hands hardened from the sword and mace, hands scarred by Arab scimitars, lived a long and happy life, peeling oranges in the luxurious gardens of Aragon. While he, whose hands retained their tenderness and had peeled oranges while brave knight and thoroughbred horse bled before the assaults of the Moors, died in pain in the mud of a leprosarium, cast out by his family and society.

Soon the whole kingdom learnt of Isabella's cruel justice and her gruesome revenge on the haughty aristocrats. Satisfied with the results, she established the title of Conte di Lepra at her court with a salary of one hundred florins.

The engine of our dark dungeon finally stopped. We were now gliding silently through the water, awaiting collision with a concrete dock. Robert opened his eyes, startled by the silence. We ought to go out to a ball and shake hands with all of Europe, I thought. Smile and extend them our leprous hands: that's what they deserved. Tenderly stroke the chubby cheeks of Viennese children and spit in every glass. Caress every tree and leave our diseased shit in every toilet. That's what they deserved, I thought, staring at the yellowish light of the big city.

The hull shook. Phantoms of boats slipped by on the Blue Danube and were lost in the oily dark of the east. We docked beside the wreck of a large cargo ship. I tried to make my heart beat faster, my palms break out in a sweat and my voice tremble, but none of that happened. There was no trace of excitement.

Robert got up slowly and went to the porthole. 'I've always wanted to see Vienna,' he said.

'I didn't know that,' I said.

'Oh yes,' came his reply.

'Let's go into town. We can go to a good hospital in the city centre. We'll get hot coffee, and they'll be fascinated to study our disease,' I said, trying to lighten Robert's mood. 'I bet they haven't had patients like us in two hundred years.'

When the Russian fist pounded on the door and then opened it and called for us to come out, as his bony fingers came in to grab us out of the darkness and make us step out into the black outside and leave the safety of the hold, then my heart began to pound: beating the rhythm of fear.

Robert got out first, and after a few angry calls I followed.

The Russian stood on the bow clenching a long wooden pole which he intended to use to maintain a safe distance between the worlds of the sick and the healthy. As soon as we started off, he pointed the pole in our direction and said, 'Nice and slow now, my friends. There's no hurry.' Quite a pleonasm, that second phrase. I sniggered and the tips of my lips quivered. Robert coughed, irritated by the cold air. The demon on the bow gave a signal and the steel turned again, now slower and slower, and I heard every creak of the toothed wheel of the iron gangway that descended towards Austrian soil and came to rest in an oily puddle. Prince Eugene the Younger, Lord of Oltenia, and his wife Constanta, I thought to myself, amused by the comparison. The bargepole poked us each in the back, and we had no strength to rebel or bare our rotten teeth. We walked down slowly, afraid of slipping and falling into the water. When we got to the end, the bargepole suddenly gave us both a hard prod and we flew towards the black puddle on the dock. Had I fallen slowly, I might have been able to see a reflection in it – of the starry sky, a plane flying to Sydney, or even The Great Bear.

The Russian threw the pole into the water and with a slow movement of his hand made the steel construction move upwards. Up, up to the heavens, I thought.

To finish off the impression, the Russian bowed low, took off his beret and gesticulated like a circus performer, as he had done several days previously when he took us on board. The mechanic's hand waved from the helmsman's cabin. Robert concluded that he ought to wave back and he moved his hand slowly, trying to establish which direction the barge had left in. I pointed to the left, to the east, but he blinked and hardly recognised my face. His pulse was weak, his forehead cold, yet he found the strength to stand up straight and take a few steps on foreign soil. He said he could walk by himself. 'Yes, of course you can!' I reassured him. I realised it was a question of pride and that Robert would obstinately limp along behind me. 'There are many steps still before you, my friend,' I said.

Before us lay the millennial dark of the Vienna Woods. The same Vienna Woods where in 1529 well-fed dromedaries and two-humped camels grazed and

Ottoman smiths, no less well-fed, devotedly sharpened thousands of yataghans, honing them for infidels' necks. This noise of this grinding, the legend says, was like the screaming of children, and there are accounts of perfumed young Habsburg ladies, in hysterical fear, seeking salvation in flight from the city ramparts.

From the depths of the Vienna Woods now came a mighty humming: the Landstrasse highway. Europe ends and Asia begins at his road. Prince von Metternich considered this dark line of cobblestones, now tarred to make asphalt, the border between two worlds. Robert and I would cross that border and continue along the roadside to the glorious city. The squeal of tyres and the drone of Volkswagen diesels became louder and louder as we passed by centenarian trees. 'We're going the right way.' I said, but Robert sat down to have a rest. 'Get up, there's no giving up now, you fool,' I told him, though at that moment I didn't know what my friend would be giving up if he waited till morning on that tree stump.

He nodded absently and tried to laugh. 'There's no giving up,' he said, getting up again.

With our hands over our eyes, we followed the movement of the glowing headlights as they veered away in front of us like ominous comets on the large Landstrasse curve. Robert made it there first. A well-compacted field separated us from the edge of the asphalt. I noticed that Robert was walking strangely, like someone who has surrendered to death's embrace and is wading out into a hail of bullets.

He was moving incredibly fast, considering his condition, and was probably in excruciating pain. Skilfully, he sidestepped stones, manoeuvring like a hunted rabbit with a fox at its heels. He seemed much too determined in his intention to reach the road.

I stopped and watched, perplexed, until I realised what Robert intended; and remembered Zoltán. Suddenly Robert shed a layer of clothing and started to run. The headlights bobbed crazily up and down, making curves of yellowish light. I tried not to lose sight of Robert and closed my damaged left eye as it was just making the landscape more blurred.

Robert slowed down and came to a halt several steps from the edge of the road. I ran even faster, trying to reach him. I began to scream out his name. Robert took off his cap, put it down on the Austrian soil, wiped the sweat from his forehead, and then raised both arms and waved goodbye. Then I stopped too. The cars' lights behind him made him a dark silhouette, a black hole in the murky microcosm of the landscape; more like the absence of a person than the presence of Robert made of flesh and blood. There was a brief silence, in which our thoughts met in the geometric centre of what people believe are long predestined fates, and then the December night's symphony of horror continued with clear acts of will, futile to resist. I stood rooted to the spot, breathless and filled with endless sorrow.

Allegro molto moderato: Robert W. Duncan slowly turns to face the river of cars and lets his arms fall by his sides. *Adagio*: He looks at the ground, looks to the left and right, to the east and west, then his eyes fall to the ground again. *Allegro molto e marcato*: His first step is unsteady; his thoughts whirl, trying to free themselves from the fetters of an irrevocable desire, a demon as strong as the north wind from the Carpathians. *La Mort d'Aase*: His second step onto the rough surface of Landstrasse, the cars honk hysterically, but the third step turns those sounds into a hard bang and a screech of brakes, into the flight of a flaccid body freed from torment and pain to land on the black of the highway.

The world went still. The earth was covered by the death of one man.

I had no trouble bursting through the crowd that had assembled round the corpse. They scattered, unable to simultaneously absorb the horror of the fatal accident and the appearance of my leprous face which I exhibited for the first time with something like pride, almost self-love. 'We are lepers... You are... swine!' I blurted out, and the diameter of the circle enlarged. I knelt down beside Robert, forgetting the dozens of staring eyes. Nor did I move when I heard the sirens of the ambulance or the crying of children on the back seats, shaken from sleep when the cars had to brake hard. Nor did any tears come, not until my eardrums were carcssed by the wonderful chords of an acoustic guitar coming from one of the vehicles. A velvet voice sang: '*I am a poor wayfaring stranger / Travelling through this world of woe / Yet there's no sickness, toil or danger / In that bright land to which I go.*'

And then... Doesn't it go on?

***

I was right. A cup of hot coffee was soon shoved through the opening in the locked hospital door. I took the cup and smashed it, and as the coffee ran down the wall it made several shapes. I recognised three species of animals, I don't remember which. The next month was full of Austrian doctors in Austrian protective suits, steel needles and pills in all the colours of the rainbow. I was told that none of the motorists, police and paramedics, who dragged me to the Mercedes ambulance had been infected with Hansen's bacillus. What luck. After his autopsy Robert was buried ten feet deep in Austrian soil. In a cemetery on the outskirts, I found out. His bones could be repatriated to the United States in three years' time if anyone was interested, I was told. It had to be that long to remove any doubt regarding the activity of the pernicious bacillus. I knew that already. But I could not have imagined that I would spend the rest of my life waking to the sound of the Adriatic Sea, to the sirens of distant ships that greet me, the devoted lighthouse-keeper.

Humane excommunication, they called it. A peaceful death in my native country. Time in abundance for thinking. Goats' cheese and luxuriant agave that blooms just for one leper. Time to take leave of life with residual memories of my days spent in the continent's last leprosarium.

I try not to think too much. Today I'm eating dried figs that compassionate fishermen from the neighbouring islands throw onto the small stone pier from time to time. There is a slight swell on the sea, the light intervals are adjusted, ships make their way to the world's harbours. The weather forecast says there will be no fog tonight. Still, I look out to sea. The Vienna surgeons removed my cataract in a routine operation but my sight remains partly impaired. When I stare at the ceiling on windy nights, plagued by insomnia, the yellow stain emits a slight flicker at the edges of my peripheral vision. My pupils rush to meet the optical illusion but it persistently avoids being seen and follows the movements of my eyeball. That elusive thing constantly levitates in the corner of the room, on the line of the horizon, near the distant fishermen's lights that skim past to the east of the rock. Sometimes it looks to me like hands or feet, I can make out the contours of a head, the features of a face, the colour of a piece of clothing. That doesn't bother me, but it frightens me. Because I realise that my imagination is gradually making a homunculus, and it is only a question of time before he comes alive. Then he will have his own movements and power of speech, his hands will be impaired by the disease and his voice may be rough, and maybe he is that very same leprous being that Robert heard when he was locked up in Room 42. So I've made a black bandage to cover my mad eye. I put it on before going to bed and take it off again when the first rays of sun disturb the gulls; just to make sure I don't go mad too.

Long walks also help. I water the wildflowers that grow beneath the window, and then go off to comb the shore. There are always traces of shipwrecks. Small things, too, can be part of big tragedies – dying crabs which the sun slowly dehydrates, an octopus with its tentacles torn off, a cat that didn't make it to the next island. I rummage in the sand with a stick and write my name among the jetsam. I wait for the waves to do their work and then walk on down the shore.

Gerhard Henrik Armauer Hansen (1841–1912) was a Norwegian scientist who in 1873 isolated the bacillus Mycobacterium leprae. Leprosy is therefore often called Hansen's disease and the bacillus that causes it – Hansen's bacillus.

Istros Books is a small, independent publisher with an eye on exciting, contemporary fiction from South East Europe. 'At Istros Books, we believe quality has no borders.'

Forthcoming titles

Nine Rabbits *Virginia Zaharieva*

Chronicling the eventful and sometimes cruel childhood of little Manda, growing up in Communist Bulgaria, this passionate book blossoms into a tale of self-fulfilment. A rambunctious celebration of food, of life and of the individual's capacity to survive and grow.

Our Man in Iraq *Robert Perišić*

A take on the Iraqi conflict from the other side of Europe, where politics and nepotism collide and the after-effects of the recent Yugoslav wars still echo throughout contemporary life.

A Handful of Sand *Marinko Koščec*

A love story and an ode to lost opportunities, Koscec's novel is a sensitive and emotive reflection on the choices we all face in life.

The Seven Terrors *Selvedin Avdić*

What starts out as a simple missing-person story soon descends into a strange underworld where reality is cracking and everyday people take on mythical roles: magical-realism Balkan style.

www.istrosbooks.com